## AN INTERRUPTED BLOODBATH

The first target had already slumped to the ground. Rosie had hit him in the chest. The second must have been a little high. Rosie's two bullets had shattered the man's skull. Then Rosie saw Rico moving up to the side of the house. Just as Rico was taking aim, Rosie pumped five rounds into him, and Rico yelled in agony. But Rosie was so intent on Rico's collapse that he forgot the villager a split second too long. Before Rosie could turn, he heard a shot. Burning, searing pain shot through his side. He'd been hit!

# THE RED MAN CONTRACT

## BOOKS BY MICHAEL MCDOWELL AND JOHN PRESTON

THE BLACK BERETS

*Deadly Reunion*
*Cold Vengeance*
*The Black Palm*
*Contract: White Lady*
*Louisiana Firestorm*
*The Death Machine Contract*
*The Red Man Contract*
*D.C. Death March*
*The Night of the Jaguar*
*Contract: Terror Summit*
*The Samurai Contract*
*The Akbar Contract*
*Blue Water Contract*

# THE RED MAN CONTRACT

MICHAEL MCDOWELL
& JOHN PRESTON

Published in 2024 by Blackstone Publishing
Cover design by Candice Edwards
Book design by Blackstone Publishing



Printed in the United States of America

ISBN 979-8-200-88200-7
Fiction / War & Military

Version 1

Blackstone Publishing
31 Mistletoe Rd.
Ashland, OR 97520

www.BlackstonePublishing.com

# 1

Roosevelt Boone thought that people were very, very stupid. Rosie had been testing that idea in the past few days. He was here in San Francisco with one of the guys. They were in this big hotel, the kind with a five-story waterfall in the lobby. Every day Rosie would come out of their room with a different outfit on.

Once he had worn a three-piece suit from a fancy store and topped it off with one of those round hats that native Africans are supposed to have. Everyone thought he was a diplomat from some "emerging nation."

Another time he'd gone down to the big cocktail lounge wearing a silk shirt open to his waist, with a bunch of gold chains hanging around his neck. The shirt was purposely tight, to grab hold of Rosie's bulging biceps, just in case anyone thought his only muscles were on his exposed chest. When the white women in that bar saw him in that getup, they were sure that he was a pro football player.

Now, in still another outfit, Rosie was walking down Fillmore Street. The Fillmore District was San Francisco's black ghetto. As though he wanted to honor the tradition of pimps and hookers who always populated the worst inner-city slums of America, Rosie was wearing a flashy suit, with the kind with fabric that seemed shiny even before you wore its fibers down to a matte-like finish. He had on a rakishly slanted hat with a wide brim. His shirtsleeves were joined with large, ostentatious cuff links with fake jewels set in fake gold. His shoes were those skinny Italian numbers with a paper-thin sole between his feet and the pavement.

He looked *bad.* He was flashing a big grin with his white teeth, egging on the pretty women—those who were selling it, those giving it away, and the silly ones who thought they'd try and keep it to themselves for a while. If he'd wanted it, he could have gotten it from any of them eventually, and he always got it for free. It was a matter of pride with him.

One reason Rosie had that luck, and one reason he could look like a pro footballer, was his big build. He was over six feet, his two hundred pounds nearly solid muscle after all the training he'd been through the past couple of years. It had been a lot of training, and it was still going on. These little visits to the outside world didn't happen all that often. It made them all the more special, and made Rosie Boone all the more anxious to enjoy all of it.

He smelled the ribs at one takeout place, and it reminded him of his childhood days of ribs and chitlins from stores just like this one in his hometown—Newark, New Jersey. Ghettoes don't differ much, one from the other. San Francisco might seem a little prettier and the weather might be a little nicer, but they were all the same—ribs and chitlins and pimps and whores. San Francisco's ghetto might be made out of pastel Victorians, while Newark's was constructed of aged brick, but it had the same poverty and ignorance, the same entrapments of drugs and prostitution, the same enslavement of police brutality and political graft.

"And the poor are always with you"—that's how Rosie's

grandmother always quoted the Bible. What she meant was: *You always gonna be poor.*

They all expected that he was going to be one of the ones trapped by the Newark ghetto. If any of them were alive, they'd be surprised. Rosie Boone could buy or sell the Fillmore District now. He got it a strange way, a unique way. It was something that had begun in Vietnam.

Rosie stopped and bought a can of Miller beer at a corner store. He wrapped it in a small brown paper bag to avoid affronting the police and began walking the Fillmore again. There were gangs of teenage boys on every corner. Poor little jerks weren't going to make it out if there wasn't a war for them, Rosie thought. That's what Rosie had—a war. It was a dirty one, one that taught him lessons he couldn't unlearn, even the ones that gave him nightmares; they weren't going to go away.

But it got him out of the ghetto. It gave him a set of skills, and those skills had gotten him a numbered Swiss bank account; a fine Cadillac car, which was sitting back on the farm in Louisiana; and a whole line of pretty high-assed black women who just loved to show Rosie how well they could spread their legs.

Rosie kept smiling at the ladies he thought might be interesting. He had something to do right now, but it would only take a little while, and then there was the entire night to entertain thoughts of sweet-smelling skin and juicy tongues and . . . *Yeah,* he smiled at a couple of women who were selling it on a corner. *Yeah.*

More kids. It was a warm night in June. The kind of warm night that brings out the kids, makes the apartments too hot, makes them fight with their daddies—if they got daddies, he thought, though more likely they fight with their mamas. Makes it easy to stand on the street and shoot the shit. The warmth makes them uncomfortable, jumpy, makes them want to do something. Makes them aware that they really have no place to go but the street. It makes them mad that they don't have some change in their pockets to go to an air-conditioned movie, makes them get ideas about how to get the money.

*Be all that you can be . . .* Rosie started to whistle the Army recruiting song. The Army had done that for him. It sure as hell had shown him all that he could be. Though he doubted the songwriter meant to be so literal, in his own case. That's because the Army had taught Rosie to be a warrior, someone who would kill and never regret it.

Rosie sat down on a stoop. The breeze off the bay was nice; it was fine. He knew, at one level, that this was warm for San Francisco, but that breeze made this city infinitely more attractive than the farm in Louisiana, where the summer nights were so hot that a body couldn't help but get sweaty and stick to the sheets. It was hard, sometimes, for the kind of woman always worried about being fresh-from-the-shower clean. You get a woman in bed in that humid heat in Shreveport and you both are going to sweat a lot. You just had to learn to get into it, to enjoy the little liquid pops that happened when a man and a woman were getting it on. You fought the smell, or you learned to love it.

The parade of people marched up and down the city street. Rosie kept on sipping on his beer. He really was making a big deal out of nothing. He was just here to score some dope. He loved good weed, and he didn't have a chance to get it back home, not with the training and all. So, since this was a vacation of sorts, he thought he might as well take the opportunity and get high. He'd also score some coke for his friend Cowboy. He should have just hit up on one of the bellhops, he thought. Didn't make any difference how high that waterfall was in the lobby—five stories or none—Rosie could always score off the bellhops in any hotel.

It would have been too easy, he decided, sipping some more beer. And he wouldn't have had a chance to dress up.

And his outfit *was* working on someone. She wasn't just a black woman; she was pitch dark, black as coal. There might be some men someplace who thought that was a turnoff, the kind of men who liked their women cocoa light. Rosie didn't mind light-skinned women, but he didn't mind dark-skinned ladies either. He just liked willing women of any hue.

Her smile was directed right at him. The light cotton dress moved subtly in the breeze. The wind seemed to want to taunt Rosie. It trapped the dress between her legs, made it hike up so tightly for a minute that he swore he could make out that special place between her legs. The woman didn't believe in any underwear.

Rosie stood up and walked over. He leaned on a lightpost near her, his elbow up at the level of his face so he could lean down. He saw her dark eyes and her smooth skin. He got a whiff of some kind of perfume, perfume that he liked a lot. "How you doin'?" he asked, flashing his teeth.

She stared at him. He couldn't understand what she was looking at so intently. Her eyes weren't focused on his—it was as though they were looking at something off to the side. Oh yeah, his earring. He kept forgetting it. It was some kind of a totem of who he had become. The small skull dangling from his ear was a part of him, and he kept forgetting it was there and that people responded to it as though it wasn't normal.

She got over her morbid curiosity and moved her eyes so she was looking right at him. "You new." It wasn't a question. She obviously felt she knew the regulars around here. Rosie smiled a little more broadly and shrugged. If she was that sure of herself, it meant the lady was selling it. Too bad.

But he wasn't going to leave her. He was enjoying himself. They bantered a little bit. "You're an awfully big man." She put a hand up against his chest. Too bad Rosie wasn't wearing his pro football outfit—maybe he could have gotten her for free if her hand had felt hard flesh and not just a fancy shirt.

"What's your name?" Rosie asked.

"Flora," she said, trying to be coy. But she'd been on the street too long to pull it off. Coyness had left her soul a long time ago. "You want a good time?" she finally offered, reverting to the rough language of a whore too fast. She should have been more circumspect, he thought.

"I do, but I think you got some extras you're going to want I'm not going to give you."

She looked puzzled.

"Like money," he explained, opening his eyes wide in a gesture that sent the same message as a shrug.

"Please?" She was whining. She did that awfully quickly as well. Junk.

Rosie stood there and scowled. The woman wanted her fix. He had plenty of money in his wallet, more than enough to take care of her for the night, and even for the week if he wanted to. But he might as well throw it down the toilet. It was just going to be wasted. He put a hand on her cheek, and she leaned into it like a house cat desperate for affection. He felt sorry for her. But, no, he wasn't going to buy junk for a whore. He studied her some more as her head moved subtly against his hand. She seemed so healthy; the shit hadn't gotten to her bad yet, the way it would. He could picture her in a few years, the youth ripped off her complexion, the flesh sagging on her bones. There wouldn't be a nice vein sticking up against her skin in a while—it'd collapse; she'd have trouble finding it.

He'd seen it happen, in 'Nam, in Newark, and there was no reason at all for it not to happen here in San Francisco. "Sorry, baby." Rosie took his hand away. She closed her eyes tight and wouldn't open them. He left her and moved down the street; he was disturbed.

There are some things you just cannot take care of. You cannot take care of the world or a whole country. Rosie wasn't the kind of man who liked to find the limits to his power, not at all. He wasn't used to finding himself up against what he could not do. He was more used to discovering what he could do—he and the rest of the guys.

He only got to the end of the corner. He went into another store and got another Miller. Outside there were more together-looking young men than most of the others he'd seen gathered on the street. He took his brown-bagged beer and went up to them. He gave them the usual street-jive talk, the language that announced he was a part of the inner circle. If they could get him the good stuff, some barely cut cocaine and dynamite dope, he would be happy to pay for it. He knew the street value of what he wanted, and he added a nice premium to it, telling them carefully that he understood the inflated prices he was offering. He just wanted a clean, quick score for some good stuff.

They were more than a little happy to hear the sums Rosie was mentioning. They broke up and moved away, since he wanted more than any of them would have carried on the street, but they knew where to go. Rosie stood on the corner; drank from his new, cold beer; and waited for them.

He calmly watched the traffic, seeing Flora down the block, out of the corner of his eye. It was really a shame. A couple of white kids came up to her, careful to park their car nearby—they obviously weren't going to walk the Fillmore this late at night by themselves for any distance longer than necessary. They were drunk. It was a shame that a nice black girl like that had to put up with white boys who were loaded, he thought.

He saw her pulling her timeless whore tricks, just as

desperate to get their business as she had been to get his. She was pleading with them at the end. They weren't going to take her. Rosie wondered why. Maybe she didn't have a place. Maybe they wanted two women. Maybe . . . He shook his head and tried to forget the whole thing.

He was not in the business of saving whores, he told himself. He just was not. He pulled on his beer and waited for his new "friends" to come back with the goods. Then he heard her scream.

His body stiffened, and his fists automatically tightened. There was an ethic here, one so fundamental he didn't even think about it. He might not be in the business of saving a woman from prostitution, but that did not mean that anyone had the right to beat her up. He threw his half-full can of beer in a trash can and walked quickly back to Flora.

The man who held her arm, yelling at her, was dressed just as Rosie was dressed. But this guy meant it; Rosie knew automatically that this was her pimp.

Now, Rosie might think it was too bad that a nice black girl had to take her body onto the street, and he might have thought she was awfully foolish to try to sell it to him, but that didn't mean he hated her. Not at all. That was all her choice. But what Rosie did hate—and he had always hated it—was some man who lived off that woman's earnings.

The first person Rosie had ever killed had tried to turn his sister onto the streets. He hadn't stood for it then, and he wasn't going to stand for it now.

"Bro, I think you should leave this little lady alone." Rosie's voice boomed loud enough so both the man and Flora froze. She was crying, still trying to wrench her arm from the man's grasp. She was also deathly frightened. She had been in trouble before, but if this stranger caused her pimp any hassle . . .

The black man studied Rosie quickly. He made a move with his free hand, trying to get into his pocket. Rosie grabbed that wrist and wouldn't let go. There was a blade inside the man's jacket; he could see its outline. "Uh-uh," Rosie said. "No equipment."

The pimp stared at Rosie. "Look, man, she's just one of my girls. She's given me problems, you know? I mean, she couldn't get you, then she scared off those two white boys. Man has to make sure his girls is doing their job."

Rosie looked at Flora, the dark mascara melting in her tears and nothing but raw fear on her face. It just made Rosie too mad. He pulled harder on the pimp's wrist, twisting it painfully. He could easily break it if he wanted to. He knew that. The man's face started to look as bad as Flora's. It made Rosie feel much better. He didn't relieve the pressure; he thought the man deserved the pain, all of it.

"You got her shit?" Rosie asked.

The man couldn't answer—his mouth was opened in a silent scream of agony.

Rosie was disappointed, but he had no choice, and let the man's arm loosen a bit. "You got her shit?" he repeated.

"Yes."

Rosie slapped his body down, found and tossed away the knife that had been in the jacket and another he found in the man's pants. In the same back pocket, he found the heroin. The girl looked at the glassine package with almost religious awe.

Her desperate need for the drug took most of Rosie's fun away. He handed it to her, then picked up the man by his collar and threw him backward, unceremoniously dumping him on a flight of stone stairs. "Get off her back," Rosie said simply.

"You." He turned to the woman. "You have any children?"

"No." She seemed surprised that he'd asked.

"Good." If there had been babies, Rosie would have done something, but now he could walk away. She was an adult, and she was making her choices, he reminded himself. He slapped his hands together, as though he wanted to get the dust of the pimp and the whore off his flesh. "If you were smart, Flora, you'd get off the street, off the shit, and away from that man. There's one fix—it'll take care of you for a while. Go find some people to help you take care of it. Do you hear me?"

Flora's eyes fluctuated between the heroin and the huge black man. There was desire when she looked at the powder and loathing when she looked at him.

Oh, shit, Rosie thought. If the woman wanted to kill her youth, how could he stop her?

He checked out the pimp. The man had been cut on the back of his head and was moaning a little, enough to make Rosie sure he wasn't going to be any trouble.

His "friends" had returned to the street corner. Rosie suddenly didn't think his outfit was any fun at all, not in the least. He wanted out of here and out of these clothes. He stormed down the block and quickly transacted his business. Then he got the first cab he saw.

The driver was relieved that he wanted to go downtown. The cabbie had enough sense to want to get out of the Fillmore.

Rosie slammed the door to the suite.

Cowboy looked up and smiled. "Hiya, any luck?" There wasn't any tension in the question, as Rosie always had luck when he went to buy cocaine for Cowboy.

But the flier immediately knew not to follow up his question, not when his black friend was in one of his moods, and Rosie was definitely in a mood.

As Rosie stormed across the large sitting room, he was not just removing his clothes but stripping them. First, he took off the fancy jacket and ripped it in half with his hands. He tore the shirt off his back with repeated motions until only a few small pieces were left hanging on his torso. He kicked off his shoes and threw them, hard, against the hotel wall. He undid his zipper with such fury that he split the trousers in half. In a matter of minutes, he was standing in the remains of his shirt collar, one sleeve, and his jockey shorts.

"Oh, you're pissed off," Cowboy finally said.

*"I am so fucking pissed off . . ."*

"Go take a shower," Cowboy responded. He went back to his book. Rosie was ready to dive across the room at the other man, then realized he did want to take a shower. He wanted to wash off the cologne he was wearing as a part of his pimp masquerade. He went into the bathroom and slammed the door just as hard as he had the other.

Cowboy had learned to take all the insanity of the other Black Berets in his stride. He had no choice. They were all so crazy, he had decided, that the idea of Rosie's destroying his brand-new clothes in their hotel room should simply be accepted as a slight personality quirk. That was all.

He heard the water running. In a short while, Rosie would start singing, which would mean the water was having its effect. You just had to learn what it was that each of them needed to calm down.

Cowboy threw his book aside and thought back over them all. They'd been together in Vietnam, where they'd met and had all become insane. There was their leader, Billy Leaps Beeker, a big half-breed Cherokee who thought he could do just about anything—and usually could. He was buying property back in Louisiana at an astonishing clip. Sometimes Cowboy thought that Beeker was trying to buy back America for the Cherokee.

Beeker you calmed down by putting him in the same room

with Tsali, the kid he'd adopted after Beeker had saved the boy's life. Tsali was a rare creature, a full-blooded Cherokee. That alone would have been enough for Billy Leaps to like him. But things happened between Billy Leaps and Tsali, things that only happen between father and son. It was as if they had wandered the earth with some primeval loneliness, something too onerous for any person to have to experience. Then they saw one another, and each saw himself and his heritage.

Put Tsali in a room with Beeker and the best came out of the man, absolutely the best. Cowboy thought that Beeker might have willingly died before he'd let his son see him weak or defeated. That must be what a son did to a man—make him want to be his best.

Of course, Cowboy had his own soft spot for the kid. But that was more like brothers. Cowboy was the one who'd helped Tsali pluck his cherry in a brothel in the Caribbean; he was the one who helped the boy hide his video games from his old man. Hell, Beeker would have liked it if Tsali and him wore loincloths all day and ate nothing but game they hunted themselves. If Billy Leaps Beeker could have wiped out all of human civilization and gotten himself and his son back to the ancient days, he'd be happy.

Maybe, just maybe, it wouldn't have mattered in those days that the kid was mute. Cowboy hated to think about that—what it must have been like for Tsali to grow up, not being able to talk, not being able to play with regular kids, getting shunted from place to place because ignorant fools thought being mute meant being dumb.

Tsali was one hell of a bright kid. Cowboy had used his own training in computers to fix up some state-of-the-art toys that allowed Tsali to communicate with the whole world. Tsali had never been upset, at least not that anyone had ever seen.

It must be like his father, Cowboy thought—not being willing to show weakness in front of his son. Maybe Tsali was afraid to show weakness or fear in front of any of them.

But if Tsali ever did get upset, Cowboy would have just put him in front of his computer terminal, sure that the boy would have been in alpha state in seconds.

Then there was Appelbaum. Was there anything other than a Louisville slugger that could make Marty Appelbaum calm down? If there were a drug on the market that could do the trick, Cowboy sure as hell wished he could find it. Appelbaum was one of those little skinny guys who just never stopped trying too hard. He was always in a state. He was always bragging about seducing women, and they were all sure that he was lying through his teeth. He was always bragging about blowing things up . . .

*That* would calm Marty down. Sure, just give him a few boxes of TNT, and the guy would be happy as a clam, happier. Marty loved to blow things up. Even in 'Nam he was the best with demolitions.

Harry could do it, too, in his own way. Haralanbos Georgeos Pappathanassiou had a special way of being able to take care of Marty. Maybe, Cowboy laughed to himself, it was just the fear that the little man would be asked to pronounce Harry's full name. Who knew?

But Harry didn't ever need to be calmed down. The huge, hairy Greek was always so low-key that no one could recall when he'd last been excited. He was hopelessly sad-looking, as though someone had done something to him long ago that he could never get over—like his mother had given birth to him and then told him he couldn't ever suck her tit. Sadness and the quiet were part of Harry's whole being.

And himself. What would make Cowboy calm when he got upset? Airplanes? No. Cowboy loved airplanes, and they excited him. Any kind of airplane. When he was in the sky, behind the controls, he was in his own heaven. His father had been a barnstormer, and Cowboy's very first memories were of being on his father's lap with a joystick between his legs. It was that intense for him.

That's the only reason he had gotten a college education. He wanted to fly jets. But they told him that he had to have a college degree to do it, so he'd gone off to Texas A&M. That's how he knew about computers too. As soon as computers became part of airplane controls, he needed to know all about them. The idea that there might be a flying craft that Cowboy couldn't pilot was too horrible even to contemplate. He had to know all about all of them.

But they didn't make him calm. Latin ladies did. A bigger smile crept across Cowboy's face. Latin ladies. He adored them so much he'd married two . . . ten . . . a dozen of them. The marriages were the best. It was all romance and kissing, and big dinners and honeymoons. It always made women so willing. But he hated being married, so he always left before the glow of the honeymoon wore off. There were all those Mrs. Cowboys down in Central America and Mexico, and probably too many of them in the United States as well.

But he had instituted a new policy of discrimination once the Black Berets had come together. There were to be no marriages in Texas, Oklahoma, or Louisiana—that was forbidden territory, too close to home.

*Home*. Cowboy sank into the couch. Louisiana was home now. They all lived on Beeker's farm near Shreveport. They'd gone their separate ways after 'Nam. None of the ways had worked. They had tried, God knows, each of them had tried. Beeker had been a schoolteacher, for Christ's sake. Harry had opened a bar in Chicago. Rosie had found work in a morgue in Newark, peeling the skin off cadavers for use on burn victims.

Marty had gotten the best of it—he'd been working in construction demolition. Cowboy had been flying, but the stakes of that kind of flying were too high—he seldom knew what his cargoes were, but the fact he had to file false flight plans and use abandoned runways in both Colombia and the United States gave him an awfully good idea.

They'd been like captainless ships wandering through life. They had only known things that made sense in 'Nam, when they'd been brought together from different branches of the services to form the most secret, the most elite, the most awesome fighting unit in Southeast Asia. Without that bond, that mission, they had been lost. They were only on target again when they had been called back together to be the Black Berets once more. They were all in their thirties now, a team again, and they knew they were going to stay that way.

Rosie's big baritone came out of the bathroom. "He's okay again," Cowboy said to the empty room. He stood up and went over to the bureau, catching a glance at himself in the mirror. Same as always, darkened glasses even in the nighttime—they were a part of him, as though the light of a single bulb would blind him. His usual shirt was a western yoke-shouldered thing with pearl buttons, and his shoes were cowboy boots, which felt as comfortable as ever.

He went over to the bar set up beside the big picture window. Outside was San Francisco, its lights bright against the backdrop of the bay. It wasn't that late. Rosie must have gotten the coke, he thought. He could toke up, and they'd go out to some nice singles place, maybe one down in the Mission District, where all the Mexican ladies hung out. They could flash their money and get laid so quickly they wouldn't know what had happened.

Cowboy poured some Scotch for himself; then, when he heard the shower water stop running, he poured a bourbon for

Rosie. A couple of drinks, his coke, Rosie would want some grass, then a night on the town, he thought.

There was a knock on the door. Cowboy left his drink and went to answer it. He pulled it open and stared right into the mouth of a Smith and Wesson Model 64. The snub-nose .357 magnum was something Cowboy *didn't* enjoy looking at.

Behind the gun were three black men. They looked as though they were mimicking the way Rosie had dressed. They wore flashy suits just like the one that Cowboy's buddy had torn off and left scattered on the floor.

Cowboy instinctively put his hands up to shoulder level. You do not fight when there's a gun pointed at your head. That is not a time for arguing. But it's always a time for quick thinking. Beeker had insisted on making them relearn all the lessons of warfare they might have forgotten.

First, most important, you gauge your enemy and his strength. Cowboy stepped back, allowing the three men to enter the hotel room, and shut the door behind them. There was only the one gun. The two other men had bulges under their jackets, but they weren't going to pull anything out right now. They were all armed, but they didn't think Cowboy was enough of a threat to worry about.

That was their first mistake. They were also surprised by him—he could tell that by the expressions on their faces. They were expecting Rosie. The sight of blond, thin Cowboy must have been a shock. That was good. They were off guard.

He listened for the sounds coming from the bathroom. Silence. He figured that Rosie was just drying off. He moved farther back into the room, carefully showing an anxious expression on his face. He was trying to remember what a white man is supposed to look like while terrified of three black toughs from the street; he was putting on a good show.

"Don't shoot! What's the problem here? Please don't shoot!" Cowboy hoped he sounded like some wimp, like a frightened bank teller. He didn't want the calculations to show on his face.

It seemed good enough. They were following him in, smiling now over the surprise at discovering him in the room and having a good time with their sense of power.

"Where's the bro?" one of them asked. "Where's the spade dude?"

"I don't know what you're talking about." Please, Rosie, don't start singing again, Cowboy thought.

He had moved them all back far enough so they were beyond the bathroom door. He commanded his face muscles to stay tense, not to show his relief. He had to redouble the effort when the door swung open. A big, naked Roosevelt Boone was ready to yell out something when he saw the four men in front of him. Instead, he just put his hands on his hips and shook his head with a disgusted expression.

"They told me there was a spade guy in here. Where is he?" the man insisted again.

There are lots of ways to take out a man. Some of them are very silent. With the care he'd take in stepping on a fly, Rosie stepped up to one of the men, who was enjoying Cowboy's cowering. He never knew what happened to him. Cowboy saw the blow coming and started speaking in a voice loud enough to block the sound of the muffling towel that was wrapped around the guy's mouth and shoved into it while one of Rosie's big hands clutched his throat *hard*, closing off the carotid arteries.

While he watched the man's eyes bug out in shock and agony, Cowboy put on his best southern accent, just the thing to keep the other two men's attention.

"I certainly do not have a nigra in this hotel room," Cowboy insisted.

The one who'd spoken snickered at the cracker response. While he was laughing, Rosie was silently laying the first corpse on the carpet. Then he moved up to the second man. Cowboy was disappointed, since Rosie was using the same technique. He'd hoped for something different, something more entertaining. Well, if Rosie wasn't going to provide it, Cowboy would have to do it himself.

The man with the gun was ready to ask another question. "Don't bother," Cowboy said. Then, with lightning speed, his leg lashed out, breaking the gunman's wrist and knocking the revolver out of his hand. The man's face had a sudden and complete expression of dismay. He grabbed his wrist where the sharp toe of the cowboy boot had landed and stared vacantly at Cowboy.

He was still staring when that same boot's sharp heel came up in a reverse kick and smashed into his chin. There was a loud crunching noise as teeth cracked against teeth and then went beyond. The jawbone was fractured by the blow and cut through the right side of the man's face; it sent a surge of blood splattering onto the white carpet.

"Messy," Rosie said in a disgusted tone of voice. "Really messy, Cowboy." He was standing stark-naked, making remarks about bad technique! Cowboy was about to get angry, then realized where the frustration was coming from.

It hadn't even been a decent fight. Hardly any fun at all. He went back to the bar and got the two drinks. He gave Rosie the bourbon. "What did you do to bring this fine example of a visiting party?"

Rosie took the bourbon and swallowed half of it in one gulp. "It was your fault. You were the one who wanted the coke."

"My fault? My fault that three assholes break into our hotel room packing rods and looking for you?"

"If you didn't want coke, none of this would have happened," Rosie said violently, accusingly. "I was just as happy sitting here and looking at some TV. But oh no, you wanted to party, so off I went, flashing a big wad of money."

One of the men had come to enough to start groaning. That annoyed Rosie, who went over and kicked him in the stomach. "Now we got this mess in the fucking room, and what are we going to do about it, huh?"

"You brought 'em here!" Cowboy insisted.

"You shouldn't have let them in the door," Rosie countered.

He smiled—he liked that one.

"Oh, for Christ's sake, Rosie, put some clothes on and get rid of them."

"Sure, boss," Rosie said. "Yassuh, yassuh, yassuh." He rolled his eyes like a bad old movie character, then kicked the broken-jawed man, who moaned again.

# 2

Cowboy piloted the twin-engine Beechcraft into position to land. Beneath their plane they could make out the house and the land immediately surrounding it. The building was deceptive. From here it appeared to be cheaply made, a simple structure of concrete blocks. It just didn't look like a third of a million dollars.

But it was. The extra cost came from the incredible reinforcements in the walls and the foundations, reinforcements that made sure nothing less than a direct nuclear attack could destroy it.

There was a large barn, but it, too, was fake. It was actually the hangar for Cowboy's toys—the Beechcraft, and soon, a new helicopter. Even the driveway that led out to the main road was constructed for double duty. It was a winding path until the approach to the central area of the farm, where it straightened out to serve as Cowboy's runway.

Not that he needed much. Cowboy could probably have landed this Beechcraft on a dirt road with a one-inch clearance on either side between the trees.

Rosie wasn't even awake yet. For one thing, there was only

the steady drone of the plane's engines, a sound he'd gotten used to long ago. For another, there wasn't any added noise from a tower. Cowboy was communicating with the ground, all right. But he was using a special keyboard to send his messages, and he was reading the replies on a small screen, where the letters and numbers marched across the green glass like stock-market quotations.

It was all a part of Tsali's nonverbal communications system. Cowboy had constructed it so the kid would be able to make contact with the men if there were an emergency while they were all out in the field. That had happened once, when he was sixteen. He'd managed to kill three intruders, who would have gladly taken him out themselves. When the Berets—and especially Beeker—came back and discovered what had gone on, they'd vowed that the kid would never be left that alone again.

The landing instructions coming over the screen were just an advanced lesson for Tsali. He was learning to fly, and Cowboy wanted him ready and familiar with all the apparatus and techniques. Cowboy could have just squatted this bird on the runway, never bothered letting anyone know he was coming, but if it gave Tsali a chance for some good lessons, he was willing to go through with the motions of calling the "tower."

Cowboy thought back to that time that Tsali had been left alone. It had been a terrible lesson for all of them, a horrible lesson at every level. He remembered how Beeker had looked while he translated Tsali's story of the three men who had come to the farm and torched the old farm buildings.

The boy had come to life once he had been found by Billy Leaps. He'd come to life and began to believe that he had finally found a place where he belonged. Then he'd seen those men torch Beeker's house. Maybe another kid with a different background and living with different men would have run away and hidden, trying only to protect his own hide. But Tsali had listened carefully to the talk of these five men called the Black Berets. He'd especially listened to Beeker and the leader's earnest belief that you protected your home, your family, and your friends above all else at all times. Tsali had those words and ideas deep inside him while he watched the destruction of the Black Berets' base.

Maybe he had no choice; maybe their lives had taken him in too much. But the kid—he was only sixteen then—had taken his only weapons—a bow and arrows and a knife—and killed the three men who'd dared to cross his path.

When the guys had listened to the story and seen Tsali tell it, they knew they were looking at themselves when they had been young and green in 'Nam. They'd been blooded at an early age as well. They had seen what they could do, the power of their hands and the control of their weapons, and they had learned that they could kill when they had to.

Now, Tsali had done it. Because he was part of them. Like them, he wouldn't walk away into a mental institution, cracked up over what had gone on. Nor would he become a braggart—Tsali didn't have to brag about that one event. Because, like the rest of them had known in Asia, it wasn't going to be the last one. There would be more.

So they had sat around a fire and eaten in silence. There were no comfortable words to give Tsali. There was little to do but tell the truth—he'd done a good job.

But they'd been haunted by what he'd gone through, haunted by their own dreams, and disturbed by what the attack meant. There was one unavoidable conclusion: someone had discovered where the house was, which meant that their reputation had begun to spread.

They had had a sinister notoriety in Vietnam. People would

hear that one of them was a member of the Black Berets and move aside. It didn't make any difference if they were Rangers or Marines, SEALs or Airborne—the Black Berets had been more than any of them. The rep was whispered about—it had never been published, it had never been broadcast, it just was.

When they'd split up after the war, the stories became mythology. Over the years, the guys would be in bars, and they'd hear about themselves, about their superhuman feats and their accomplishments. Probably the only surprising thing about it was the element of truth retained in some of the tales; there had been some remarkable incidents.

But they'd learned a lesson during the war. A reputation can backfire. You become the big guy on the block, and someone out there is going to want to shoot you down. Now, if three had tracked them to the farm in Louisiana, it meant there would be others. In some unknowable network of international agents and mercenaries, big-time intrigue and bigger-time crime, there was a new element: the Black Berets were back from the dead.

They were always on guard after that. Tsali's communications network had been a part of it, but so was the incredible security system and the rule they almost always followed that the farm never be left unguarded. The house, their home, had become a real fortress. It was ready for outside attack.

It had made them draw closer together, made them stronger, more of a unit. The pettiness between them had receded. Like any team that survives, they'd learned to work together, acknowledge and appreciate each other's skills and strengths, compensate for one another's weaknesses.

Like in that hotel room. All the hotshot talking and jiving Cowboy and Rosie had with one another as they'd disposed of the three intruders was a show. In fact, Cowboy had trusted that Rosie would know what to do, just as Rosie had trusted Cowboy to know enough to draw the men farther into the hotel room so he'd have a shot at them.

No matter what else they'd say to one another, they both did know that it had really been Cowboy's fault. He should never have let the men in. But it wouldn't have done any good to have just sat there and blamed the flier. The only real response was to make up for his mistake with quick action, and Rosie had done that.

Just as the Berets should never have left Tsali alone in the first place. They knew it had been their fault that he'd drawn blood at such an early age, their fault that he'd been left to defend himself and the house alone. It was their responsibility that some of those few remaining moments of boyhood had been taken away from the kid.

The tires of the Beechcraft hit the ground with a chirp of burning rubber. Rosie woke up with a start as the plane slowed down on the driveway-runway. They were back. He stretched, his seat belt still holding him into place and his body movements utterly relaxed. He trusted Cowboy to get them there. That was the flier's business—to do the transporting.

What would ever happen if that trust left? Cowboy wondered as he taxied toward the hangar. Too heavy. Alone they hadn't been able to make it in the world before. Now they could. They'd make mistakes, sure, but they'd bring things back together again, learn their lessons, and go on. They could only get closer, tighter. They couldn't break their circle and end up back out there, separated and alienated, again. They just couldn't.

The engines were cut, and both Cowboy and Rosie unbuckled their belts and climbed out of the plane. They had stored their stuff in the aft baggage compartment and now went about pulling it out.

Cowboy kept looking toward the house, expecting Tsali to come running to greet them after the landing. The kid had grown up too quickly, but he still knew his buddy Cowboy would bring back some kind of present after a trip to a city like San Francisco. That, at least, was one element of adolescence that Tsali still was allowed. But there was no movement for a while, and then, when the door did open, and Tsali started to walk toward them, he did it with a slow gait and an air of seriousness.

Cowboy had put his bags on the ground. Now he lifted a large but light package from the compartment. It was wrapped in brown paper. He waited to see some light on Tsali's face—this was obviously his gift. There was no response.

Have we made him so old so quickly that we've lost even that? Cowboy wondered.

He watched the teenager as he approached. He'd gained weight after the past two years of a good diet and even better exercise. Tsali always held something back, as though he still wasn't sure that they weren't going to send him out to some new foster home. After all, for his entire life before being with them, that's what had happened. Whenever he'd get comfortable and begin to like the woman of the house or learn to get along with the other children, it seemed the social workers received a special signal to yank him out.

So, he was always trying to prove himself, even after it was utterly unnecessary, so far as the Black Berets were concerned. He had driven himself into the ground to do everything each of the Black Berets wanted of him. He'd run with Beeker, flown with Cowboy, shot guns with Rosie, wrestled with Harry, learned demolitions from Appelbaum.

Now it was all showing in the broadened shoulders and the deeper chest. When Beeker had found Tsali, he had been skin and bones. Cowboy had seen him the first day, with bandages covering wounds rednecks had inflicted upon him. He could have counted every one of the ribs on the boy's body.

As Tsali stepped toward him, and used a sign-language greeting that Cowboy returned, the flier realized that Tsali might already weigh more than he did. It was only the long, shoulder-length hair kept in the traditional Indian style that was an unmistakable part of the old Tsali.

Even the smile was gone now. Cowboy had to shake himself loose from the depressing thoughts. This was too much. The kid was too sad. "Problems?" Cowboy speculated.

Tsali took a deep breath. *Yes*, he signed back.

"Shit." All Cowboy needed or wanted was trouble on his return. "Come on, take that package for me." He indicated the wrapped parcel. Then he put his arm around the kid's shoulders, and they walked back to the house together, with Rosie bringing up the rear.

When the door had slammed shut behind the three of them, Cowboy took in the assembled group. It certainly did feel like trouble. They didn't even look up. Usually, Marty would be all over them, worrying about how many women they'd seduced, as though the voyeuristic pleasure could make up for his own lack of success. Harry would have cracked a smile at least, and that crack, coming from Harry, who so seldom smiled, would have spoken pages. Beeker should have been angry. Beeker *always* managed to be angry at times like this. They were late, or he was sure they had broken the training rules about drugs, or they had spent too much money, or . . . There was always something for Billy Leaps to complain about.

Instead, they just sat there like silent judges. "Well, I am *so* glad to be home," Rosie boomed out from behind. He was as displeased with their reception as Cowboy was.

No one spoke. They dropped their luggage on the floor and moved to the table. It was a huge baronial dining table. The house was well furnished, but there weren't many pieces as large as this one. There were seats around it for just the five members of the team and Tsali. There were some couches around a fireplace at the other end of the room, and a state-of-the-art kitchen on the opposite end. All three areas were in one open space.

This one room held the only evidence of the extraordinary wealth they'd accumulated. There was a single corridor off it. Lining it were six sleeping cubicles. Each one had only a single bed, a bureau, a nightstand, and a reading chair. It was all a man really needed. They shared a communal bath with a group shower. It resembled a barracks more than a house, which made them more comfortable, especially in the beginning.

When Cowboy, Rosie, and Tsali had sat down, the flier started to speak. "So, Marty, what happened, huh? Your pecker fall off? You, Harry, what's your problem? You find something to make you too happy? Beeker, you—"

"Shut up," Harry said. If it had been an event for Harry to break into a smile, it was remarkable for him to speak to any of them that way. Harry was the one who could stand to be in the same room alone with Appelbaum, for Christ's sake.

Cowboy and Rosie exchanged glances. This was heavy-hitting shit, whatever it was. It was obviously not a time for them to be joking. "Okay," Cowboy followed up cautiously, "something is going on. Now, I've just been away with our good friend Roosevelt Boone, and we've been to an air show in San Francisco, and we don't have a fucking clue what it is. Want to fill us in? This is a team, remember? One for all and all for one?"

Beeker slammed his hand down on the table. "I gotta do something, and these two are acting like it's the end of the world. It's just something I gotta do."

"You and Tsali," Harry corrected, and there was bitterness in his voice. Anger and bitterness from Harry? Both at once?

"Mr. Cigar Store Indian thinks he has the right to go out

on his own fucking mission without us. Thinks that we have no place in it," Marty complained.

"That's not it." Beeker wasn't speaking with his usual forcefulness. "It's just that it's something I owe someone. It's Indian business. It's a debt I have to pay off. And there's no money in it; it's something that you can't get anything out of."

Harry spoke up again. "Except maybe doing something for a friend."

"Can I get a straight answer? Huh?" Cowboy was incredulous that these men were acting this way. This was something he'd never seen.

Tsali stood—it would be the kid who broke the ice—and went to the kitchen counter. He retrieved a letter and handed it to Cowboy. The letter was addressed to Beeker in handwriting that was barely legible. It was block writing, the kind a first grader might use.

He opened it up and read it aloud, for Rosie's sake.

> Dear Billy Leaps,
>
> Look, remember me? White Wind Smith? You know, LeJeune. Guess you won't forget that. I got trouble, bad trouble. I am back on the reservation, out in Nevada. The Anglos are doing us in. You once said anytime. Well, I think anytime is now. Will you come?

There was a scrawled signature on the bottom: *Sgt. White W. Smith.*

"So, what does this mean?" Cowboy asked.

"We did all the checking we could. The guy's a member of the Coyote Clan, a small tribe out west. They're the ones who have been in the news lately. Did you see that?" Harry was giving the information as quickly as he could.

Rosie did remember something on the news. "They're the ones who have the legit claim to all that land? The ones the courts just ruled on?"

"Right," Marty said. "They were on this godforsaken reservation, see, and now it looks like the feds fucked up their treaties—they aren't valid. The Coyote Clan actually owns most of Nevada and chunks of Arizona, California, and Utah along with it."

"That doesn't sound like trouble to me," Rosie said. "Hell, it sounds like they pulled one over on the whole world. Man, if they're smart—smarter than us—they wouldn't settle for some acreage; they'd go for condos on the beach. Trade it all in for money, honey."

"You don't trade holy land for money," Beeker sneered. "That land is holy to them."

"Stop, don't get off the story. Now, they won in the courts. They have the land. So, what's the problem? What's this talk about a mission alone, Beek?" Cowboy asked.

"I owe White Wind. That's all. He says he's in trouble. And so does Delilah."

Delilah was their contact in Washington, a woman so mysterious that they never had learned where her connections really came from. But her connections produced the best intelligence in the country—they'd learned at least that much.

"So, when Delilah says there's trouble, we go and take care of the trouble. We always have, and we always will. So, what's the plan?" Cowboy didn't hesitate. He meant what he was saying.

"Beeker wants to go alone. He thinks it's *just* an Indian problem," Harry answered.

"Beeker, there is only one kind of problem: a Black Berets problem." Rosie was clenching his own fists.

The team, Cowboy was thinking. We cannot break up the

team. A strange cold sweat broke out on his skin. It was something he hadn't experienced in a long time; a primal kind of fear was producing it. He now knew why Harry and Marty were so angry and upset. They were feeling it as well.

"You never said that Rosie should off and go to Africa to settle a black problem, or that I should have been the one to go to Texas that time to settle a Texan problem. What is this shit, Beeker? Are you losing it?"

Billy Leaps wasn't looking him in the eye. "This is different."

"How?" Cowboy demanded.

"Because . . ." Beeker couldn't find his words.

"Because you're an Indian and we're not? Because we're not used to reservations? Because we won't know how to act? Because you have to save the whole fucking Indian world by yourself?" Rosie suggested the whole line of excuses, each one of them in words dripping contempt. "Would you let me go into the ghetto alone? Would you let me tell you that you would be an embarrassment? Hell, you'd just look funny. But you might have a role somewhere else to let me do your stuff and use it."

"This is self-interest. There's no reward—"

"Reward? Beeker, remember me? I'm the one who takes care of our books. We're all millionaires more than once. We have gotten our rewards. We're *fucking rich*! We are also a team. What good's all this money if we're not doing the things that we have to do—need to do—for ourselves?

"We buy new cars, I buy new airplanes and computers, we go on trips, we have a good time, and then we go and work. But work doesn't have to pay for the rest of it anymore. Not anymore."

They sat in silence. Cowboy's speech didn't seem to do any good, except to make him sweat harder.

Tsali stood up and went over to his father. He nudged him

for his attention. His hands flew so quickly that none of the rest could follow the conversation. Beeker suddenly said, "No." Tsali's hands flew again, with an added expression of tension on his face to underline something. Cowboy watched and saw that expression and knew what it was—it was the same thing sending clammy sweat down his armpits. It was fear.

"No," Beeker repeated.

For a second, Cowboy thought the kid would cry. After he'd watched the boy go through the hell of that initiation a couple of years ago, after he'd seen him torture himself with training that'd break most men, after the things the boy had witnessed with stoic responses, Cowboy had thought tears would never flow down his face. But now they were threatening. The hands were moving again.

Beeker was clearly unhappy. But Tsali had pinned him on something the rest of them hadn't. "Okay, we're a team. We have different strengths, and we might need all of them. Tsali and I will go in first. It's perfect cover. We can—"

"No, I'm going with you. Someone is going with you," Rosie insisted.

Tsali's hands flew again.

Beeker shrugged, then shook his head with frustration, "All right, all right. The three of us—Tsali, Rosie, me—will go in. We can handle that. You three will stay put. *That's an order.* When we've found out more about this, we'll send for you."

"Now," Cowboy said with an honest surge of relief, "you sound like a Marine sergeant again."

# 3

The hot, dry wind swept across the barren land. It wasn't quite the Sahara—there were a few trees to be seen, and grass grew in patches. There was even an occasional flower that broke the monotony of the beige dirt and rock. But it was dry; it was barren; it was more like a movie director's idea of a moonscape than a part of the United States.

Beeker and Tsali got out of the rental car and stood in front of it, beside one another. The reservation town they were standing in had little to do with the modern motel they had just left.

There were two rows of small, dilapidated shacks along the one street. There was one larger than the others, apparently a general store, according to the sand-worn metal signs that advertised Dr Pepper, Arco gasoline, Bayer aspirin, and a host of other goods. Once the signs had been bright primary colors, but now they were all the same near-beige. There was nothing untouched by the windblown sand in this part of the country.

The motel twenty-five miles away had artificially grown trees around it that had been kept alive by trucked-in water. The same trucks had kept the swimming pool full and clean. There had been a bar with fake wooden paneling, and a restaurant that served steaks and chops. From the looks of the raggedy kids playing in the one street, it had been a long time since they had eaten a steak, if ever. Their bellies were distended, curving out in a bulge that was the most undeniable evidence of malnutrition.

Beeker put an arm around his son and drew him close. This was their heritage. Beeker remembered scenes like this all too well. His whole childhood had been made up of them. So would Tsali's have been if he had grown up on a reservation. As much as Beeker hated and loathed the Louisiana social service workers for all the hell they'd put Tsali through—the foster homes, the juvenile detention centers, the workhouses—at least they couldn't send the kid across the state line to that place of living death called the Cherokee reservation.

All the smells of that place came back to him. The sounds of the men roaring drunk on cheap whiskey and the women roaring angry at them for it. The honky-tonk music that came from the speakeasies, where the men ruined their bodies and the women threw theirs away.

He could vaguely recall his own mother's constant attack on the degenerate Cherokee. "A nation of warriors," she would laugh as she spat at the body of an unconscious drunk along the roadway. "A people of honor," she would sneer.

Then she'd go to the same bars and drink the same cheap whiskey and spread her legs for those same drunks. His father had tried to fight it, and he'd succeeded. Both his parents eventually left him. His mother gave Beeker only one gift—his blue eyes. But his father had saved him. His father had created the one and only way out for him.

Beeker's father had run away, according to his own mother, the grandmother who would bring up Billy Leaps Beeker. He'd joined the Marines. During the Korean War, on some hill so unknown it was only identified with a number, not even a name, Beeker's father had died with a belly full of Communist bullets. But he'd died as an *honorable warrior*. It was as though he'd given up his life to show his son that the words that were used with such disdain—*warrior* and *honorable*—had meaning. There was an option besides a slow death of self-hatred.

Beeker had savored that lesson. He'd listened to his grandmother talk endlessly about the history of the Cherokee. He took in all he could of her wisdom and her learning, except her admonition never to follow his father's path. That, she claimed, wasn't a Cherokee way. It wasn't a Cherokee path to fight with modern weapons in foreign wars that could only benefit the white man who had twice raped the Cherokee, first driving them from their ancestral homes in the East, then stealing their Oklahoma land when it was discovered to be sitting on something more than waste, when it was discovered to sit over rich deposits of oil and gas.

Beeker wouldn't listen to that part of the old woman's ranting and raving. He would take her hatred when she looked with scorn at his blue eyes, and he would forgive her when she couldn't help but be angry with him. His very existence reminded her of her dead son. But he would never give up the dream of following his father into the Marine Corps.

It had been a fantasy that had sustained him, nurtured him, gave him strength and that one elusive element so many Cherokee children could never grasp—hope.

Beeker looked at Tsali and thought of all the things he might be giving his adopted son. Hope, he prayed, was one of them. He slapped Tsali on the back, and the two of them walked down the street toward the general store.

They walked up onto its wooden porch and opened the screen door. There was a wave of sour smells that came from the place. Hygiene wasn't high on the storekeeper's list, nor was stock. When they scanned the shelves of goods, they saw dusty cans and some packages so old that there were people back in Shreveport who would have loved having them as collector's items. Beeker's eyes caught one whole shelf of baking goods whose decorations he was sure he'd seen in an antique store back East, when Delilah had insisted on a day's shopping.

There was only one person in the shop, a white man. He was sitting behind the counter, his belly grotesquely swollen with beer. Malnutrition wasn't this guy's problem. Beeker walked up to him. He nodded to the small square of locked boxes beside the cash register. "You the postmaster?" Like so many small towns in America, the general store obviously doubled as the postal service delivery point.

The man was reading a copy of *Sports Illustrated.* He looked up, obviously not pleased to be distracted from his reading. He evidently first saw the olive complexion of Beeker's skin. Another Indian. He wasn't going to move quickly on that account. But he saw something else as well. It might have been the new, clean clothing. Beeker was only wearing a pair of khaki slacks and a plain cotton shirt, but they were obviously fresh from the cleaners. There was that, and the severe haircut, the short high inside. Even if you didn't know it was the insignia of a Marine, it was a look that commanded a certain respect.

He stood up—the effort wasn't minor, that was obvious. "Yeah, you want some stamps? You want to rent a box? You're new here."

Beeker looked at the fat man and saw the dried evidence of his breakfast crusted on his shirt. He saw the thin legs and the sticklike arms. He checked himself—there was no reason to let his man know how little Billy Leaps thought of him. "No, just some information."

"Yeah?" The man was on guard. "What kind?"

"I'm looking for White Wind Smith. Know where I can find him?"

The storekeeper-postmaster returned to his seat and picked up his magazine again. This was just an Indian. "You can find him down the street—the yellow house, the one with no number on it. Maybe three doors that way." He pointed in a southerly direction, but his face had already returned to his reading.

Beeker stood there and felt a surge of anger go through his body. He didn't care if an idiot like this fat Anglo wanted to believe his color made him a better man than an Indian. But he was furious that Tsali would have to see this kind of ignorance close up. He was ready to move forward and take the situation into his own, give the man a taste of something more painful than words, but he felt his son's hand on his arm. It laid there gently, but its touch was as binding as a strong man's.

Tsali signed something with his free hand. *Asshole.* Then he nodded to the entrance. His facial expression made it obvious he didn't want to stay. Beeker nodded. The kid was right. He was often right, astonishingly so.

They walked down the street, Beeker glad to breathe some fresh air after the stale interior of the store. They came to the house the storekeeper must have meant. There were traces of yellow paint left on the front wall. It was tiny—there couldn't be more than two rooms inside. Beeker walked up to the door and knocked. A voice called, "Yeah, a minute. Who is it?"

"Beeker."

The sounds of the body inside moving around stopped suddenly, as though it was shocked. "You serious?"

"White Wind?"

The body was moving faster, so fast it knocked something over. Out of the dark, a hand came and yanked the screen open. "Am I glad to see you." The man who gave the greeting was supposed to be the same age as Billy Leaps: thirty-seven.

The two men stared at one another as though they were going back through the years to LeJeune. Boot camp, the hell they went through to prove to a bunch of cracker drill instructors that Indians could be Marines—not just that but that Indians could be the *best* Marines.

White Wind had that same look of nobility about him. Tsali could see it. He was studying the other Indian man, and the action seemed to make him stand a little taller himself. Even in the doorway to this hovel, even with old and worn clothing on, White Wind was the kind of man his father was.

The two were still. Tsali almost expected them to salute one another. Instead, White Wind eventually broke their silence by extending a hand. "Welcome to my house." He and Beeker had shook quickly, then White Wind stood aside. Tsali and Billy Leaps walked in.

The house was poor, there was no doubt about that. There weren't any new store-bought tables with coordinated chairs. Instead, there was a Formica dinette with a mismatched set of seats ringing it. Off to the side was a couch covered with a cheap cloth, the upholstery too worn to be sat on without that slight protection. The kitchen area was off to one side. It was a small room with a gas stove. This larger room was for both sitting and eating. There was another doorway. A single bed could be seen there.

At first glance the house might seem to be a study in American poverty. But both Beeker and Tsali could sense something else. It was immaculately clean. It was cared for as well as it possibly could be. Even the decoration—a single magazine page with a portrait of John F. Kennedy—was perfectly placed on one wall. Only tape held it up, and maybe the placement was to cover a hole in the plaster, but it was centered, the tape carefully aligned.

If White Wind was ashamed of his poverty, he wasn't going to admit it. With graciousness he pointed to places on the couch for the two visitors. Only after they'd taken their places did he bring one of the chairs from the Formica table and put it in front of them for himself. Before he sat, he asked, "Would you like some coffee? Can make it real easy."

"No, thanks. We ate just before we came."

White Wind didn't argue. He took his seat and sat ramrod stiff. Tsali knew that posture. It was partially Indian, and the rest was Marine Corps. It was the same combination of traditions he saw so often in his father.

"Billy Leaps, I'm glad to see you. I need you."

Beeker answered with the same stiffness, almost formality, "I'm glad I could get here. I'm glad you asked me."

"There's trouble." White Wind pronounced those words with no emotion. "You know about the court rulings? The case that the Coyote Clan won?"

"Yes."

"Beeker, the whites, they don't want to give it up. They want to keep it all for themselves. The politicians, the miners, the Army, all of them. They lost in their own fucking courts, Beeker, and they won't give it up. There's going to be trouble. Lots of trouble. Some people, they're going to get hurt. The wrong people are going to get blamed."

"Tell me about it," Beeker said. That Anglos would resist giving Indians back their land wasn't news to him. What they might do to resist, that was something else.

"We got it all back in court. I'm on the tribal council." That was no surprise; White Wind was a war hero, which wins elections. He also had the bearing of a leader. "We know we can't just go around and kick people off land they've been squatting on for over a century. We know there're some things we want to continue. The mines. Hell, some of them can go on. We just want fair payment for the ores they're taking out. There's oil. There's coal. There's lots.

"And we'll let them have their towns. It should be easy. You know, a negotiation. We get some money, build some schools with it, educate some kids, get a hospital, get back some of the holy ground and all. We'd be happy."

"They won't do that?" Beeker was surprised. Indians had won legal suits against Anglos as far away as Maine. The Indians had gotten bigger reservations, a few legal concessions, and a whole lot of cash money. "Why won't they give in?"

"We don't really know. It's getting worse, Billy Leaps. Violence is erupting."

"White Wind, you didn't get me all the way out here to stop a couple of fistfights. What kind of violence?"

"There have been bombings at the mines. A couple of bad ones. It's a miracle that they haven't killed a whole lot of people yet. There have been some vigilantes who attacked one of the towns in the reservation. They left a couple of guys badly beaten up . . ."

"And?" Beeker could tell that White Wind was having trouble with this story. He was looking at the floor again, wringing his hands.

"They raped some of the women."

"Anglos?"

"The vigilantes, yes. The bombings were supposed to be done by a radical Indian group. The Native American Crusade."

"But you don't believe that?" Beeker knew his friend didn't.

White Wind sat upright in his chair. His hands rested placidly on his lap. "My son is the head of the Native American Crusade."

*And your son wouldn't endanger innocent miners.* Beeker

looked at his old Marine buddy. He thought quickly about all the kids gone wrong in all the different ways they could. What would keep a hot-blooded Indian youth from bombing a mine? Why would White Wind question that his son's anger might not have gotten out of hand? He sensed something stir beside him. Tsali.

A man has to assume that his son is going to do the right thing. He has to. And he has to trust that his friend's son would too.

"What does this crusade group want?"

White Wind looked at Beeker with a sudden ease. "They want justice."

"Then they'll get it."

# 4

White Wind had given them directions. Beeker cursed the whole way up the rutted-out road. He should have known to rent a four-wheel drive, he thought. At least he should have gotten a car with a standard transmission. The station wagon had looked good—that was the only thing you could say about it. It was big, its engine powerful, and it was having a hell of a time climbing up the road that led up the mesa.

Billy Leaps had seen the grand mesas in the Hopi and Navajo country. They had been beautiful—you knew why those people had believed gods lived in them. But this one in the middle of the Nevada wasteland was just an extension of the monotonous flat plain below. It was the same dull color—the rocks had no beauty, no grandeur. The vistas were noticeable only because they were so extensive. You could see for miles and miles from here. But there was nothing impressive to see.

Tsali was studying it intensely all the same. He knew better than to bother his father while the man was driving over this difficult terrain. He was just staring out his window, watching the land go by, noting the few plants and fewer trees. The car, surprisingly, made it to the top. The road stopped its incline all of a sudden. There, in front of them, was the tabletop of the mesa.

It wasn't that large—a couple of miles in circumference at most. But it was obviously the place they were looking for—the village White Wind had said there'd be.

This one was only a few thousand yards away. It was strikingly different from the one where White Wind lived. There were no wooden structures here, no general store with faded evidence of American commercialism. This was the real thing.

Beeker parked the car, and he and Tsali got out and started to walk toward the collection of rounded buildings constructed out of the earth. It was made of a type of primitive adobe material, the shape more like a Navajo hogan, a half circle over the ground.

Tsali was anxious to explore this—Beeker could tell. The boy wouldn't run ahead, but he would've liked to. This was going to be one of his first experiences with a traditional Indian village.

There were lots of them around the country. More and more all the time. Many had been started for the sake of more tourist dollars, that or for more respect from the tourists. If they insisted on intruding on Indian life, at least they should see the real thing and get some meaningful lessons.

But some were started by the young bloods who were disdaining the Anglo ways and wanted to return to the old values. That's how this one had gotten started. White Wind had begun to tell the story, but Beeker knew he'd learn more by coming here himself and looking at it.

It was probably Tsali's long hair that kept the small group of men and women from being upset at their approach. His obviously Indian features and shoulder-length hair made a clear announcement that this man and his son were approaching without threat.

One of the men came out to greet them. He wasn't on

guard, but he wasn't going out of his way to be friendly either. Beeker had gone to a couple of the Indian get-togethers held in places like Gallup, New Mexico. He'd been disgusted with the way some people would approach the traditional ways and then back off, returning to some form of European prudity.

One of the most striking ways men had shown that was to wear a loincloth, the simple piece of clothing old warriors wore in good weather. But that was too little for the television-educated Indians of Gallup. They'd put on black swimming trunks underneath. Whoever this man was who approached them, Beeker knew he wouldn't condone that kind of compromise. He wore a regular loincloth, a pair of leather moccasins—obviously handmade—and a chest plate of small animal bones. That was all.

His hair was long, even longer than Tsali's. It was blowing in the soft, hot wind. "You looking for something?" he asked.

Beeker gave White Wind's son's name: "Small Eagle Smith."

The man looked at him for a minute. "Drop the Smith out here. We don't use that shit. I'm Small Eagle." He didn't put out his hand in greeting.

Beeker could see the resemblance, not so much to the man he'd just left but in his memory of the jarhead he'd gone through boot camp with. Small Eagle looked like his father twenty years ago. That must be his age right about now, he thought—twenty. Maybe a little more. Yes, he remembered, White Wind had fathered a son just before he enlisted. That wasn't a big surprise. Lots of young Indians start families early. This kid was squawking at his mother's nipple while his father and Billy Leaps were facing up to the DIs at Lejeune.

"I'm Beeker. Billy Leaps Beeker. This is my son, Tsali. We're Cherokee."

Small Eagle studied them. "You the guy my father's always talking about?"

"Yeah. We knew each other."

Another hesitation. "I hear good things about you. I grew up hearing good things about you in the letters he'd send home from the war, then in the stories he told when he returned. You made a better hero than the cowboys on television." Small Eagle was smirking. "Course, you did learn to say more than 'Yes, Kemosabe.'"

Tsali was laughing his silent laugh. Small Eagle looked, puzzled at the way no sound came from the boy. "He's mute," Beeker said, no sound of reproach in his voice.

"Come. Into the village. You're as welcome as any stranger would ever be."

The three men moved to the collection of buildings. There were six other adults waiting for them. Small Eagle introduced them all quickly, using their traditional names and not mentioning any modern ones, if they had any. Beeker nodded to each one, then shook the hands of a couple of men who offered theirs to him. He was taking it all in, but he was more impressed with the children playing on the other side of the tiny village. They were also in scant traditional dress. But their bellies weren't distended, and even if they were only wearing small loincloths, they were laughing and enjoying themselves with an energy that had been missing in the reservation town. They, at least, were being well fed and cared for.

There was food cooking on a fire. Small Eagle invited them to sit down. Animal fat was boiling in a heavy pot. As the men spoke, one of the women was pounding dough with her bare hands and tossing the flattened material into the oil. It puffed up, probably leavened with some natural ingredient. Within a short number of minutes, it was ready to be turned. The newly exposed cooked side of the bread was a rich brown. The woman took it from the fire and was ready to put it aside. Then she saw the wonder on Tsali's face. She couldn't resist handing him the still-hot bread.

He took a bite, and Beeker smiled. He remembered the wonderful taste of that stuff—his grandmother used to make it at home. There had, after all, been good things to remember about that part of his life, and he was glad now that Tsali was getting some of it.

Small Eagle was watching Beeker. "What's the big hero doing out here? You got a way to cut in on the land settlement?"

"You're awful quick to expect people to want something," Beeker said.

"It's something you learn on the reservation. Seems that people who aren't from here are always looking to take what they can, what little there is. You seen my father?"

Beeker nodded that he had.

"You saw that store, then? Samuelson's? It makes that slob crazy to think that there might be a member of the Coyote Clan with a dollar bill in his pocket. *Crazy*. Doesn't make any difference how little they are or how big. They all get mad if they think the Coyote Clan has anything they can't get their hands on."

"What's making the big ones upset?" Beeker knew that was the real question.

"Oil. Coal. Land for grazing hundreds, thousands of head of cattle and horses. Water for California cities. You name it. With the court settlement, the Coyote Clan has a lot. It just means we have a lot bigger Samuelsons in the world to hassle us."

Small Eagle reached over and took a piece of the hot pan bread. He ripped a piece off and chewed on it.

"White Wind said you were in trouble."

Small Eagle kept on chewing while he looked at Beeker. "If you think that I blew up those mines, you're wrong. I don't want to fight anyone. This group of us"—he swept his hand to indicate the small gathering around the fire—"just wants to live here in peace. Have a little more things, a better chance to save our water supply, less bother from the government. But we're not after anyone. We're just prepared to keep this mesa.

"You know, that's why the treaty case went our way. Did they tell you the details?"

Beeker hadn't bothered with the fine print.

"See, the federal government sent troops to 'pacify' the Coyote Clan over a century ago. The warriors fought them. They fought them to a standstill. They were never defeated. They withdrew up to the top of this mesa. There used to be a well that gave them water. They had a cache of supplies here.

"They could defend this table rock against a whole army. No problem. So, there never was a treaty. That's the whole case. The Army gave up. The Coyote Clan came down off the mesa and reclaimed their ancestral homes. Without a treaty limiting the definition of that homeland, they had a legal right to their original Spanish grants."

Small Eagle smiled. "All the times the federal government fucked over an Indian tribe were made up for right here on the mesa. We won. Maybe just once. But we won. Maybe it took a century and more. But we won."

Beeker looked at Tsali. The boy's eyes were glistening. He loved hearing this story. After hearing about all the defeats and humiliations, there was one victory. What did that mean to a youngster? Probably just a simple thing. There was a moment of nobility, and a flicker of hope. A touch of history to be proud of, a hint of a future to build for. Powerful stuff.

"Who is causing the trouble, then? Who's doing the shit?" Beeker asked the question forcefully. He trusted this young man.

"The Samuelsons of the world," Small Eagle said. "Find yourself a general store that wants to make money off the Coyote

Clan, you'll find trouble if you tell that man he's got to leave. Which store is the center? Maybe the biggest—Nevari Minerals. Maybe the ugliest, the sheriff and his sister-in-law, the state senator who thinks it was a terrible thing that the Coyote Clan council went to court—ungrateful of them to bite the hand that'd fed them surplus hog meat all those years, the kind of meat with more fat than anything else, the kind that makes a baby's stomach hurt.

"I don't know, Billy Leaps Beeker. I just know there's trouble."

"Why are you up here now? Why now, when your father thinks you might be a target, you might be a part of the trouble."

"My father thinks I'm part of the problem?" The idea obviously hurt Small Eagle. "No, no, I'm not. But, see, there's some strength here. This is where we won, like I told you. This is the place we won. From here, where we can recreate the old ways, a message can go out. The people can have dignity. The people can relearn their heritage—"

"You teaching the people how to use guns?" Billy Leaps said, interrupting Small Eagle before the man went too far off on his political trip.

"No. But maybe we should."

"We'll see." Beeker stood and signed a message to Tsali. "I'll be back. Later."

Small Eagle studied him. "Yeah, you will. You'll be welcome."

# 5

Beeker never would have chosen to stay in a motel with a name like Coyote Head Inn. But in this part of the country, it seemed there wasn't a single commercial establishment that didn't try to rip off the Indians.

The inn was a basic American roadside motel with swimming pool and steak house. If you could ignore the plastic decorations and the heads of Indians on the walls, you could have imagined yourself in Peoria or Providence, Savannah or San Antonio. They were all the same.

Beeker walked into the motel bar and found Rosie sitting with a tall glass of bourbon in his hands. The black man saw the scowl on Billy Leaps's face and fended off the attack he knew was coming. "Just one, for Christ's sake. It's not as though there's an armed enemy out there."

"How do you know?" Beeker demanded. "You're probably blind drunk. You wouldn't see one if it was looking you in the face."

Rosie knew he'd made a mistake with his attempt at rationalizing his drink with the leader. As soon as Beeker was off the Louisiana farm, he was convinced he might as well be back in the jungles of Southeast Asia. There was a foe around every corner, or, at least, you should act like it.

"Well, now you're here to protect me if there is one. Hell, while you've been out sightseeing all day, I've been cooped up in the fucking library and the goddamned newspaper office. You've been having a ball with your old buddy, while I've been in the only places on earth that are drier and less comfortable than this damned desert."

Rosie defiantly sipped at his drink. He did it slowly, savoring it, knowing he wouldn't get another so long as Beeker was sitting here with him. "What'd you get?"

Beeker and Tsali had sat down. Beeker waved away a waitress, but then saw his son's fallen face. "Two colas," he ordered. "What did you get?" he repeated.

Rosie smiled. "I got some amazing social change. You wouldn't have believed what these people have managed to do in the past year, since the probable court verdict came to light. They got this sheriff in this county—"

"I heard about him," Beeker said.

"Mike Passak. This man makes a Georgia redneck look like his skin is pale pink. At least, he used to. Once upon a time, he would put any Indian on the street after dark in the drunk tank as a matter of principle. Now, he's talking up the noble past of the Native American." Rosie chuckled over the obvious hypocrisy of the lawman.

"The whole thing's repeated at every level. *Every* level. The newspaper itself used to write about the horrors of living so close to a reservation, like it was something that decent Americans shouldn't have to smell if the air's blowing in the wrong direction. Now, the reservation is an opportunity for partnership between the races. *Brotherhood* is taking on new meaning in the *Mesa County Gazette*. They got this skirt that's a member of the state senate, Cecelia Range? Well, she used to say that the traditional dress of the Indian men—what they'd wear at a public powwow or whatever they call it here—was an obscenity. She got your pal's son thrown in a detention home 'cause of some kind of diaper he wore once—"

"A loincloth," Beeker corrected.

"Whatever it was, could have been a caftan for all I care. But she used to be on this moral crusade against nudity in the Indian culture, not wanting Anglo kids to be exposed to the Coyote Clan youngsters, 'cause they didn't have proper ethical attitudes. Now? Hell, she'd walk down Main Street in a tutu if she could get reelected."

"So their attitudes have changed. What about the bombings? The rapes? The vigilantes? This isn't much to show for a whole day in the library, Rosie."

"Look, Beeker, you gotta understand. This *Mesa County Gazette* is about as trustworthy and honest as a chamber of commerce mimeographed newsletter. They only give out the good stuff the way the proper citizens see it happening. They do that, but that's the limit.

"The whole thing stinks. The bombings got big play—all the usual about private property being sacred among civilized people. You know the rap. But no one hurt. It had to be timed pretty carefully, as far as I can tell. There's only a half shift when there weren't men in that mine. They even made sure that a couple of inspectors weren't in there. I can't tell about the actual bombs; you'd have to have Appelbaum—"

"Not yet. I'm not ready for Appelbaum yet," Beeker pronounced. Marty would drive them all nuts if he was here.

"You're going to need him, 'cause that mine is the center of the whole thing. There's answers in that mine, Beeker. I just know it.

"The rapes, they got reported on the comic page. Seems the prevailing wisdom, even in these renewed days of the noble savage, is that any Coyote Clan woman who gets it must have wanted it. No one took that seriously, except your friend's boy. He came down and got a network television reporter all hot and bothered about it.

"The paper called it, 'One of our own turning against us.' You aren't supposed to bring notice to Mesa County at any cost. Not for bad publicity. It might have made the six o'clock news somewhere else, but the story stayed with the funnies here.

"They don't talk about vigilantes much in the paper. I don't think they ever even used that word. I could see it—I could even taste it in the way they wrote about things. But if you didn't know the way they all communicate that, you wouldn't have found it."

Beeker studied the full glass of cola the waitress had silently delivered to their table. "There must be something else."

"Lots. Lots of bucks. Big ones, all over the place. A lot of people are going to lose a lot of money if the Coyote Clan takes all their land back. It's a time to pick your enemy. Ranchers, they're a good bet. The mining companies—"

"Which ones?" Beeker asked.

"Nevari, that's the granddaddy. At least around here. Almost all the multinationals got a finger in the mineral pie in this part of the country. But I doubt they'd play as dirty as Nevari—it's got all its marbles close by."

"It was their mine?"

"That blew up? Yeah, it was their mine."

Beeker thought some more. "It's time to call Shreveport. Time some things got moving."

# 6

Mr. Sherwood Hatcher sat across the desk from the personnel director of Nevari Minerals Corporation. The office was in a gleaming tower in downtown Los Angeles. It was furnished in the best taste that modern American companies had adopted this year. That made Mr. Hatcher feel very good about working for Nevari. Usually, it meant that a firm was raking it in if they could afford to constantly redecorate to meet the challenges of the latest wave.

Mr. Hatcher was trying very hard to make Nevari Minerals want him just as bad as they wanted the sleek furniture. It was easy for him to do that. Nevari was obviously an affirmative action employer. No less than the personnel director herself was able to fill two slots for them. She wasn't just a woman. She was a *Latin* woman. Maria Vasquela.

It was a shame that she was being so strictly formal about their relationship at this moment. There were much better things to do than to ask pointless questions about Mr. Hatcher's former employment. But she insisted upon it.

"These are very impressive credentials."

*And those are very impressive tits*, Cowboy wanted to say, but he held himself in check. He remembered just how striking his résumé was. Delilah and her connections just never ceased to inspire him. He had only made a single call to Washington, and there were all these pieces of paper on Maria Vasquela's desk. It didn't even occur to him to doubt that each and every one of them would check out. Delilah didn't make mistakes.

"We do in fact have a need for a corporate pilot. The opening only just came to my attention."

How did Delilah do that? he wondered. There must be limits, but Cowboy wasn't going to test them. Maybe she just broke the guy's legs. "Well, isn't that just great? I mean, for both of us."

"It is certainly a pleasant coincidence, Mr. Hatcher," Maria said, but without a smile.

He nearly corrected her on his name, but then remembered that he was indeed "Mr. Hatcher." Every once in a while, Cowboy would look at his pilot's license and wonder how his had been switched on him. Then it would dawn on him that this same name, Hatcher, was on his birth certificate and on his driver's license as well. He was so used to being Cowboy that his given name was alien to him.

But for the attentions of a woman like Maria Vasquela, ah, for her, he'd be Señor Hatcher any day. He wondered if she was married.

"I'm sure this will check out. But the formalities, you do understand," Maria said with a sound of resignation. "It's Tuesday. With any luck, I could have all the necessary verifications in my office by Friday. Certainly, your license is in order. If I can reach your last three employers, call the FAA office—"

"Oh, I'm sure you'll have no problem with any of that." Knowing Delilah, there was some little cog in the federal bureaucracy sitting in some office building in Washington with his very own computer monitor ready to take and answer any call having to do with the man named Sherwood Hatcher.

Cowboy knew he had to do this carefully as he leaned forward. "My only problem, Ms. Vasquela, is that I'm so lost in a big city like this one."

Maria frowned. "Mr. Hatcher, you just moved here from New York?"

Fucking details! "Well, but that's a different kind of big city. I mean, Los Angeles *sprawls* . . ."

Maria wasn't receiving his meaning. "Would you like a map?"

"I was hoping"—Cowboy leaned farther over the desk, thankful that his sunglasses would hide the naked lust in his eyes—"that I'd find a guide."

The message was received. Negatively. "Mr. Hatcher, I will proceed with the details." Maria Vasquela stood up. "I see that you're staying in a residential hotel in the Hollywood district. I'm told many showgirls live there as well. You may find yourself a . . . *guide* there. In the meantime . . ." she held out her hand. "Good day."

Cowboy knew defeat when he faced it squarely. He stood and refused the hand, instead just lifted the brim of his Stetson. "Thanks much, Ms. Vasquela. I'm looking forward to a very healthy working relationship."

"I'm sure you are."

At least he'd discovered that the Nevari corporate planes were located at the West Orange General Aviation Terminal. Cowboy decided he might as well drive out there. If he couldn't get laid on a Tuesday, late afternoon, at least he could look at airplanes; it was always the next best thing.

The orders from Beeker had been both direct and puzzling. But then, this was the start of an operation. They were in the field, so far as the Black Berets leader was concerned. In the field, you don't take time out to hold a little consciousness-raising meeting with your troops. You give orders and your troops obey.

Cowboy's orders had been clear. He was to call Delilah, get a way to insinuate himself into the corporate structure of some company named Nevari Minerals, and move his ass to wherever it was necessary. He was to gather information, fast. Cowboy knew that didn't mean paperwork. That would already have been done. It meant the inside stuff.

Ms. Vasquela would have been perfect. He shouldn't have been so anxious just because she was Latin. If she had been as old as his mother and as Swedish as a reindeer, Cowboy should have found the way to get into her pants and keep himself there. Pillow talk was the most efficient form of industrial espionage.

He pulled into the parking lot of the airport and climbed out. It was a typical general-aviation operation. Some of these places were larger and busier than most commercial airports. These were the fields used by the private planes so dear to the American corporate heart. No waiting in line for seat assignments for these executives, no getting bumped or worrying about making a connection at Dallas-Fort Worth or O'Hare. Time was money in the boardroom. The best way to buy time was to own your own planes.

It wasn't the biggest, but West Orange wasn't the smallest either. The actual terminal building was larger than the one in Shreveport. He walked over to it. There was a full lobby here, a waiting area for the executives while their chauffeur-pilots taxied up to the convenient gates. Wherever you have company officers important enough to warrant private planes, you have men who like to spend their free time in a bar.

The Propellor Pub was off to the side. Cowboy decided he could start there. He'd never allow himself to fly after drinking, at least not from a public field. There was too much danger of losing his license. But today it would be fine.

It was happy hour by now. The pub was getting crowded. Cowboy went to the bar and took a stool. He ordered a tequila and lime from the harried bartender.

When he had his drink in his hand, he swiveled the barstool around and took in the crowd. It made him check his watch. Just after five. That explained it. There were a lot of ground workers in the pub. The crews must have just gotten off work and stopped in here for one on their way home.

He looked for a friendly face. Cowboy, like every other professional pilot, had great respect for ground crews. They were the ones tightening the bolts on the plane he would have to fly. They had to make sure the tanks were filled with the correct fuel, and the necessary maintenance was performed on time. Sure, he could do almost all of it himself.

He knew all the planes he flew regularly. But on a busy schedule, you had to have a good crew to trust.

It was another team.

Damn, and he wished he could be alone. Just him and a lady. He thought about that, all these dependencies. He was mortally dependent on his ground crew. Then turn around and his life could be in the hands of the other Black Berets; it had been more times than he wanted to remember. Then there were all those emotions. Worrying about Tsali. Worrying about the ladies after they got married. Worrying that he had planted a kid in their wombs—*Oh no!* He stopped himself. That was one of the most dangerous of all his thoughts and fears.

Whenever he thought about the heavy shit that went on between Tsali and Beeker, he started to think that maybe there was a little Cowboy down there in Central America, and he started—*Oh no!*

He downed the whole of his drink and waved to the bartender to fill it up. "A double," he decided this time.

Then he saw her. She was blond, but given the rest of it, he'd overlook the one problem. Her hair was cut short. It framed her tanned face perfectly, setting off the clear green eyes. Her lips didn't seem to have on lipstick, or if they did, it was that natural kind, the type that just made them seem wet, not colored. Her body . . . Cowboy sipped his drink. Her body was just *fine.*

It was the clothing that was making him all the more amazed. Because the big decal on her right breast—that beautiful, full breast—was clearly announcing her employer. "NEVARI MINERALS." This Nordic goddess was his ground crew.

Well, if God wanted him to be dependent on other people, at least he was doing a damn good job about picking his partners.

Cowboy stood and pulled some bills out of his pocket to pay for his drinks. Then he walked over to the table where the woman was sitting, talking to a couple of other women. "Uh, may I introduce myself?"

The blonde looked up. Her expression was speculative. Used to this kind of come-on, she was checking Cowboy out. "You can. What good it will do you, I don't know."

Cowboy smiled. "It's the logo, Nevari. I'm probably going to start flying for them next week. I thought you could fill me in on some details."

"Details?" She smiled now. "You want me to do the filling in?"

*Contact!*

It had been a fine dinner. Fine. The drinks and the wine had flowed. It turned out that Samantha was more than able to keep up with Cowboy in that department. They'd gotten a good buzz on, and they never did talk about the motel. It just became a joint assumption at some point in the evening.

It was close by, cooperative about the lack of luggage, comfortable, and the bed was enormous. As soon as they'd walked in, Samantha had spread out on it on her back. She held up her arms. Cowboy needed no more invitation than that.

He lowered his body on hers, and their lips met. His arms snaked around her waist and lifted up her midsection. He could feel her grind under his hips. The sensation of her slow circular movements was wonderful. He could even imagine for a while that she was Mexican or Honduran. Honduran—that would have been better.

Her tongue pushed his lips apart and moved into him, licking at the top of his mouth, sucking a little bit here, her teeth biting a little bit there. He made a motion to spread her legs farther. He merely had to hint. She was more than willing to comply.

Her legs came up over the back of his thighs. Their message was complete and unmistakable. He didn't wait for any more invitations.

Their clothes flew off, thrown into all the corners of the room. "Don't you ever take those off?" she asked when they were both naked. Cowboy hadn't even thought about his dark glasses. "Oh yeah."

He put them carefully on the bed stand. Then their naked flesh touched from neck to toe and their mouths found each other again. Hot and cold, fast and slow, they changed their energy time after time, egging each other on so much that the liquids from each of their bodies began to spread out over their skin. It was an excruciating self-discipline for him, probably for her as well.

She was the one who finally made the ultimate move. She pressed up on his chest, motioning for him to roll off her. He was aching hard and thought she meant to climb on, and he wasn't going to have any complaints about that, not in the least. He would be *fine* with that.

He complied, putting his hands up behind his neck, perfectly willing to let her do all the work. Her mouth moved down his belly, and now he saw that she had a different scenario in her plans. He closed his eyes, waiting for that moment. Suddenly, his head was so full of anticipation that his cock felt cold. It was just there waving above his belly and waiting.

She lingered on his navel, tonguing it deeply, teasing him so badly he thought he'd lose his self-control. But then, just when he thought he'd have to do something about the tension building up inside him, it happened. It happened, and it felt like his whole body was engulfed in a hot bath.

Hell, if Samantha knew how to take care of a plane's engine half as well as she gave head, they were going to make a wonderful pair.

"Don't you ever talk about anything besides business?" she pouted later.

The motel had thankfully been large enough to have room service. There was a cooler with two bottles of the best champagne in the house beside the bed. Cowboy reached over and grabbed the one open bottle and refilled their glasses.

"Want me to tell you that you have the most sensual tonsils in the world?" he asked.

She played at frowning at his joke, but the bubbles rising in the glass were too alluring. She sipped the wine. "This stuff makes me silly," she said, wrinkling her nose against the effervescence.

"I just want to know the other people I'll be working with. I already know you and me are going to get along fine."

She was staring at the champagne. "Wouldn't you rather talk about how strange it is for a girl to be on the ground crew? Everyone else thinks it's strange."

"Nah. I mean, women are everywhere now. And I love

planes; I'm never surprised when someone else wants to work around them."

For the first time, Cowboy saw that she had finally had too much to drink. Maybe she was just tired from all the fun and games they'd had. But her eyes were fixed on the glass, watching the bubbles of the wine. "It was 'cause of my daddy," Samantha said. "He loved planes. He never could have a little boy, just girls. One of us had to do something that would make him happy."

"That makes you a very fine person, Samantha." Cowboy hated himself for the way he was treating her, taking advantage of her drinking. He watched her down the whole glass and hold it out for a refill. He obliged. The guilt wasn't *that* bad, and the information had to be gotten out of her.

"Well, Mr. Adamson sure thinks so. He told me so just the other day. Mr. Adamson likes me."

Cowboy watched the wine disappear again and poured still more. "Who's Mr. Adamson?" he asked.

"You jealous? Already?" The smile on her face showed she wasn't upset by the idea.

"Every man is always a little jealous of every other man, Samantha."

"Yes, I know. I think sometimes that Mr. Adamson would like to be my daddy. I think he's jealous of my father. But that's okay. Mr. Adamson's okay."

"Who is he?" Cowboy pressed.

Samantha seemed startled by the question. "Him? Why, he's the president. He's a good friend. He likes me. Sometimes he lets me go on little trips with him—you know, the day trips." She smirked. "He keeps me on the payroll, and we . . . you know, in the plane."

Cowboy leaned over and took one of her large pink nipples in his mouth. As he rolled it around with his tongue and listened to Samantha's hurrying breath, he realized he was going to be a bastard. He was going to use and misuse this girl's affections. He was going to wring all her inside information out of her and then drop her.

He was a bastard all right. He knew it. He also knew he was getting hard again. *Ain't life a bitch!*

# 7

The mine foreman looked at the two applications. He kept looking up at the unlikely pair of men standing in front of him. "You guys have a lot of experience."

"Yeah, we're the best. We're the baddest. We live to go underground. Man, the sun hurts my eyes. I mean, I hate daylight. I just love to—"

The bigger man threw an elbow into the blond runt's chest. "Yeah. We work hard."

The one who'd just spoken was impressive. He was huge. His hair was jet black, and he had a heavy nose. The hair on his body was poking up from the front and the back of his shirt. He was incredibly quiet for a man that large. There wasn't any kind of laughter in his voice. He spoke in simple, direct terms. He would be a good worker—the foreman knew that at once. The kind who did his job day in and day out, never complained. He was one of those guys who you looked at after he had a couple of days off, and you wondered what the hell he did during his spare time. It was inconceivable that he was really happy doing anything besides physical labor.

Jim Kanton liked that kind of man. "Harry the Greek," he joked. "What are you, a bookmaker?"

The dark man spun out some impossible number of syllables that began with something like Harambol . . . Jim would never be able to pronounce all of that, and he knew immediately why the guy used a nickname, even on an employment form. "Yeah, well, we've got to be able to check your references."

"It's all under Harry the Greek. Even my union card says that. If you really want it, I can get out my birth certificate."

"No." Jim looked at the union card. If that little piece of paper was made out that way, then his own ass was covered. He'd hire this one right away.

It was the other guy who bothered him. "Marty Appelbaum?"

"Yeah, man, I'm the best." The little man was almost jumping up and down. He was moving so quickly that Jim was sure his glasses would fall off if he didn't calm himself.

"You want to work on the demolition crew with Harry?" Jim just couldn't imagine trusting this man with the sticks of explosives necessary to work a mine. Just looking at him was making Jim nervous.

"Hey, Mr. Foreman, I don't just know about explosives. I *am* explosives. I *am* the detonator. I *am* the—"

"He's okay. We work together." The Greek guy spoke again. He said the few words looking directly into Kanton's eyes. He meant them.

Jim sighed. You had to go with first impressions. Especially in an operation like the Nevari mines. The pay might be union scale, and union scale might be hard to get these days. But it was still the wasteland of Nevada. And it was getting more and more difficult to make men work under these conditions. That freak explosion hadn't helped recruiting. Word of a mine explosion moves fast and furious through the grapevine. No one wanted to go underground for a company whose track record included that kind of fuckup.

"Okay. Looks good. Company policy says I got to send these forms to headquarters before you can be permanent. They got to check you out. But I can take you on temporary—just mechanical work. You get full wages, no benefits. When this comes back, say in two weeks, you go on regular payroll. For demolitions. *If* it checks out."

"Oh, it will. That's going to check out better than you'd ever believe, isn't it, Harry? Tell the man how well it's going to check out." Marty Appelbaum seemed to think this was a funny joke.

Kanton was puzzled, but the Greek guy just said, "Don't worry. See you tomorrow."

"You got it."

As the odd couple walked away, Kanton wondered how the hell they'd ever gotten together. What kept them with one another? Sometimes you just couldn't understand.

A couple of hours later, at a honky-tonk bar on the state highway near their rented rooms, Harry was wondering the same thing. Marty was downing double bourbons. The little man seemed to be able to drink untold amounts of liquor, and it just didn't make any difference. He never seemed to get drunk.

Even the very few times Marty had tried drugs, they never seemed to have any effect. He just kept on talking, kept on bragging, kept on goading, kept on and on and on . . .

"Harry, you think we're going to get some real action on this one? Huh? I'm tired of all the pussy stuff we got to do all the time. Stay home and guard the house. Go off to some gook island and off some guys and then go home before we even get a chance to get laid.

"Pisses me off, Harry, the way the rest of them get all the

good stuff, and we're left by ourselves. Man, I bet you Cowboy and Rosie aren't drinking in some fucked-up bar with two old whores and a hundred miners getting drunk. I bet they're dipping their sticks in some well-oiled cans right this minute . . ." Marty went on and on and on . . .

Harry had developed a knack of seeming to listen to every word Marty said with great care and concern when he really never heard a single thing. He just sat and drank his beer. Marty's part of the charade was to never notice when Harry just stood up in the middle of one of his sentences and wandered away to take a piss or get another drink.

It was perfect for both of them. Marty could say any lie he wanted to believe, and he could believe that someone was taking him seriously. Harry could look as though he listened, and because it appeared that he was in the middle of an intense conversation, no one else ever bothered him. Harry hated to talk to strangers. Harry hated to talk.

Harry stood up in midsentence. He walked over to the bar and waited for the big-breasted bartender to notice him. There was a single man to his left. He was wearing a large felt hat, badly used and beaten down. It had a feather stuck in the hatband. His nose was prominent and his skin more than a little weather-beaten, but the hue was too dark to have gotten just from the sun. He was obviously Indian.

Harry nodded to him. The guy nodded back. Harry liked him. He liked him because he didn't say anything, just acknowledged Harry's presence. That was all Harry ever really wanted from a guy.

It wasn't enough for the two men on the other side.

"Isn't that pretty. All our government quotas in a row." The man who spoke was about Harry's size, except his belly was twice as round. He was blond, but his skin was pockmarked.

"We got the red man quota with Big Arrow, and we got the fag quota with the hairy ape. Or is he the hairy ape quota, and his friend's the fag quota? Who knows who the government'll send down in the mines next?"

The bartender came over to Harry and took his order for another Coors and two double bourbons. He caught the worried look she gave the two men beside him. It was pretty obvious she was used to their causing trouble in the bar.

She moved as quickly as she could to fill his order. She wanted him out of there as soon as possible.

"You think this one gets cornholed by the Jew runt?" the man continued.

"Nah, Ron, it don't happen that way. I heard the foreman say this guy's Greek. You know what that means. Hell, I was in the Navy. Everyone in the Navy knows what it means to be Greek. And they love kikes too."

Harry closed his eyes. It wasn't that he cared what these guys were saying. Words from this kind of scum just flowed off his back. But if Marty ever heard someone talking about him being—

"Hey, come on, Harry. I got some stuff to tell you. I just thought of a great way to—"

"I bet you did, Jew boy. I bet you did."

Ron really shouldn't have said that in that way. Harry knew he just shouldn't have said that. If he adds—

"I bet you figured out a way to plow your buddy with your tiny kike cock and not fall in."

*Oh no.*

Harry reached into his pocket and pulled out a wad of bills to pay for the drinks that had just been delivered. He saw the panic in the woman's eyes as she stood on the other side of the bar and watched. She'd probably never seen anything like it. It was always so strange.

Harry could picture exactly what was happening. It was totally predictable. It happened anytime that anyone was stupid enough to make the double mistake. It was a bad mistake to make. First of all, you never, *ever* made anti-Semitic remarks to Appelbaum. It made him remember his grandparents who'd died in Treblinka. He hated that.

Second of all, you never, *ever* called him a queer. Marty could not stand being called a queer, and it made him furious. When you put the two of them together, it was all over.

First off, he did just what Harry could hear him doing now. He started to hyperventilate. Too often people laughed when he did that. Marty was so skinny and seemed so weak and unable to take care of himself. That was a major miscalculation. People had fallen into the false idea that only big, big men were strong. There were little men like Marty who had so much strength in their bodies, bodies that didn't have an ounce of unmuscled flesh, that they could do remarkable things with their physiques.

The hyperventilation would have been a good trick for a guy like Appelbaum to learn if it wasn't natural. It made him look foolish. But if you knew him, then you realized it was something like a little train building up steam to climb up over a big mountain. It needed lots of steam; it needed to build up pressure.

Harry took a swig of his Coors and figured that it was time for Marty to ask the question.

"Are you calling me queer?"

Marty was sort of a gentleman about that one part of it. He always gave his opponents a chance to back off. It was very kind of him, Harry always thought.

There was Marty's chest going again, heaving up and down, as though the oxygen he was taking in and expelling could stoke up his engine. He could picture it, the little ribs pushing out, sucking in, pushing out, sucking in . . .

"Let's just say the closest thing to eating pussy you've ever done is chewing on a tuna fish sandwich," Ron replied.

Okay, Harry thought to himself, now count to five. *One, two, three, four . . .*

*Aaargggghhhh!*

That was Ron. Marty usually took out the first one with a boot to the balls. Harry never figured out why Marty always did that, but he did. There was no use criticizing him for it; it always worked. Harry took another drink.

Ron's friend would make a move right about now.

Ooommmmmppppphhhh!

That would be the old head in the belly routine. Marty used that one a lot.

*Bang, bang, crack, bang, bang, crack . . .*

There went the friend's ribs. Marty always did a little dance on one of the guys. Usually, the boot in the balls kept them down and out, so it wasn't necessary to use it on them. But the ones who just got the head in the stomach were often only winded. The dance could put them out of commission for a long time if Marty got to, oh, about five or six ribs.

*Crack.*

That should just about do it.

"Marty, I'm going to drink your bourbon if you don't come and get it."

There was sudden silence. "Hey, that's my booze."

Only then did Harry turn around. He'd gotten it down perfectly. Ron was passed out on the floor in a fetal position—even in his unconscious state, he was desperately hanging on to his balls. Marty was standing right on the chest of the other guy, whose head was rolled onto the floor in just the right position for a little trickle of blood to spill out.

The crowd around them was agape. They'd never seen

anything like this before, not some little, tiny guy take out two bullies without any help and apparently without any effort.

Harry sighed. He turned back to the bartender. "Another Coors, and you better call an ambulance. Internal injuries—it could be nasty."

She nodded once. First, she brought back the beer. Whatever these guys were, she wasn't about to argue with them. As soon as she put the bottle in front of Harry, another hand came out and put down two crumpled dollar bills to pay for them. It was the Indian guy. He didn't say a word, just nodded, walked over to the table where Marty and Harry had been sitting, and took an empty chair.

"Harry, where's my booze? I'll tell you, that sure took a lot of energy. I mean, come on, Harry, did you see me? Huh? Did you see my moves? I had them down in two seconds flat."

Harry was going over to join his new friend. Marty was following with his barrage of exaggerated description. Harry nodded to the Indian and sat down beside him.

"Harry, it was great." Marty was aware that people were watching him. He wasn't satisfied with simply sitting down. He turned a chair around so its back faced the table and then straddled the seat—he thought that looked more masculine. He'd seen John Wayne do it in a western movie once and had never forgotten it.

"Harry." The Greek put out his hand to the Indian.

"Big Arrow," was the only verbal reply. The man put up his hand in an almost vertical position. Harry took it, and they clasped hard, using lots of pressure, not as a challenge to one another but in a kind of manly appreciation.

"You'll be in trouble soon," Big Arrow said. He nodded toward the area of the bar where the crowd was beginning to get over its surprise at what had happened and was starting to talk about it. It was the kind of buzzing conversation sure to produce some idiot who'd try to prove his stuff by getting Appelbaum into another fight.

Harry sighed. This was all just as predictable as the rest of it.

"Got some beer at my house. Not far," Big Arrow said.

Harry shook his head quickly. "Come on, Marty. My friend's invited us to his place for a nightcap."

Appelbaum downed the remaining double bourbon and smiled his maniac's smile. "He got some skirt there? Huh? I could really use a piece."

The other men didn't reply, but silently stood up. Marty wasn't pleased. But, as always, he followed Harry's lead.

# 8

Cowboy certainly did wish that Maria Vasquela would remember that Mexican women were supposed to be hot-blooded. He was behind the controls of the Nevari Minerals' flagship, a Lear Jet with all the speed and comfort a pilot could want.

Of course, his credentials had checked out. They had been tailor-made for Nevari's requirements, and Vasquela had little choice in the matter. Cowboy was the new top-dog corporate pilot.

That didn't mean she had to treat him like shit. She was in the back of the plane talking to the creep Adamson. Cowboy had instinctively hated the man. Maybe, just a little, because the guy was putting it to Samantha and playing little girl and Daddy games with her. Maybe because he was a good soldier on alert, and automatically could spot a bad guy.

Adamson was that kind of slippery character who looked as though he had been born in one of the three-piece pinstripe suits he always wore. Cowboy just couldn't imagine the man in diapers any more than he could imagine him as a youngster. Adamson had probably suffered through his adolescence, dreaded his twenties, and his thirties must have been torturous. But now, in his forties, he would be happy. There's a certain kind of man who has to hold power and authority, and there are some kinds of power and authority that can only come with age. Adamson was finally old enough to get it all—the presidency of a major corporation, the power of money, and the age to play Daddy to a nubile young woman.

The Lear Jet had just taken off. They were gaining altitude. The flight to Mesa City wouldn't be long—an hour and a half. Cowboy flicked on the intercom to the passenger compartment and listened. Maybe he'd get some valuable information. Maybe he'd just get hot and bothered listening to Vasquela and Adamson making time.

The intercom was designed for those constant FAA messages pilots had to give passengers, even the ones who had bought the comfort of a private jet. Cowboy had convinced Samantha that it would be great to fiddle with it a little bit, make it a two-way deal, supposedly so he could listen to her and the boss playing their little games back there. He'd told her it'd make him hot. That way, he'd said, he could join in on their fun.

She'd thought that was endearing. They'd rewired the Lear together the day before Cowboy formally received his employment notice.

It was a lot less interesting to listen to Adamson and Vasquela than it had been that one time the boss had been making it with Samantha. It had been even sexier than Cowboy could have imagined.

But Maria Vasquela wasn't going to provide any comic relief or pornographic inspiration, that was for sure. She was just going to be the cold-steeled businesswoman she presented herself as.

The conversation that came through Cowboy's headphones was boring, as boring as a French chef broadcast. The analytic speech was as bad as listening to Beeker once he got on his

Marine high horse and started mouthing off about rules and regulations.

There was a need for five class B miners in Mesa; they could be transferred from Installation 775C in Arizona. The cost was significantly less than retraining, and besides, they could avoid Nevada State Regulation 5C-101.

Cowboy daydreamed back to Samantha's little rap about her "daddy" taking care of her and her helping her "daddy" to the bathroom. She'd held "it" while he made "pee-pee," and then she went, "Ooohhh, Daddy, look! It's getting big."

That had been outta sight. Just imagining blond Samantha milking old man Adamson's had been both hilarious and erotic.

"Of course, there's the special personnel request. It's most difficult, Mr. Adamson."

Cowboy smirked when he heard Maria's voice making that statement. What did Adamson want this time? A French governess with a hairbrush for his butt?

"Hardly difficult, Vasquela. There are plenty of men with those qualifications in our employ. It shouldn't take much to find the necessary numbers to make up the bulk of the complement of men that's necessary."

"Of course. It just means disregarding our personnel policies. It means ignoring security. It means—"

"Ms. Vasquela, those rules were made for my benefit. It made the paperwork easier and more efficient. I choose to break those rules. It is your job to carry them out."

Maria's hiss could be heard over the intercom. Cowboy knew that this Mexican lady did not like to have her holy structures tampered with any more than she wanted her body toyed with. "As you wish."

"That's right—as I wish. I have to have fifty men ready soon. If the recruitment's really a problem, get ahold of Sheriff

Passak. He'll know about any drifters around Mesa City who would know how to handle a gun. Hire them."

"Yes, Mr. Adamson." Maria sounded like the very efficient executive again.

Drifters who know how to handle guns for the Nevari payroll? Cowboy thought that over and couldn't come up with any answer that sounded good *at all.*

"Remember, Vasquela. They're to be on a dummy corporation payroll. Take their names off Nevari's computers. They should cease to exist so far as we're concerned, at least as soon as they've taken this assignment. I don't want a single trace of their Social Security numbers, their medical insurance, not a thing to link them to us."

"But, Mr. Adamson, what will we do when it comes to reporting the taxes? When they come to claim their benefits?"

"Listen, Vasquela, you'll find a way. You helped yourself find a way at Transnational Banking Corporation, don't forget that. I just want you to be able to use those same skills for me. Just as I used my skills to remove you from a potentially . . . embarrassing situation."

My, my, thought Cowboy. We got a recruiting drive going on that's made for Rosie, and we got a little something that might make Maria Vasquela a lot more cooperative. He flicked off the intercom.

He started to whistle. This was a very worthwhile trip, and the two-way communications were just what the doctor ordered. He'd have to find a way to thank Samantha.

# 9

The steam in the hogan was sweltering hot. Beeker watched as Small Eagle leaned over and threw some more water on the smoldering rocks. There was a sharp hiss, and a new cloud rose up to fill the small space.

The room wasn't as oppressive as a real sauna. That would have been more than a man could bear for a long period of time. This was part of the ritual cleansing of the Coyote Clan. Small Eagle had invited them to come to the ceremony. Beeker knew it was really for Tsali. Small Eagle, for whatever reason, hadn't really come to trust Beeker. He would have trusted Rosie less, but the young leader of the Native American Crusade had known a real convert when he saw one. Tsali had been entranced by the way the Coyote Clan people were living here on the mesa.

Through Beeker's ability to translate his sign language, the boy had asked countless questions about traditions and the way of life of the Coyote Clan people here in their hideaway. Small Eagle might not have given Beeker the time of day, but he'd spent untold hours answering Tsali's inquiries.

It was a regular thing for the Coyote Clan to honor the full moon with a gathering and a feast, in their meager use of the term. The men of the clan went to these observances only after they had shared a communal time in the sweathouse.

There were four men besides Beeker, his son, and Rosie. All were naked and utterly unconscious of that fact. They were sitting around a tier of wooden seats that ringed the hogan, the fire in the center. Off to his side, Beeker could see that at least two of the Coyote Clan men were in a trance.

He knew it was drug induced. He'd taken Small Eagle aside at the very beginning and warned the young man that life would become unpleasant for him if Tsali were ever initiated into the drug use of the tribe.

"It's part of the old religion," Small Eagle had objected.

"If you want to practice any religion, you keep my son away from your joy seeds. I don't care if they're organic. I don't care if my grandfather used them. I don't care if your mother swears by them. I know damn well what those things are. You want to trip out like some hippie in San Francisco, you go do it. You just leave my boy out of it."

Small Eagle had argued, but Beeker had been unyielding. For whatever reason, Small Eagle had never used the drugs himself in front of Beeker. Maybe he wanted to stay in the same mindset, Beeker thought, just in case his lack of trust proved correct.

Right now, so far as Beeker was concerned, all the other Coyote Clan could be blissing out into chemical land; it was fine by him. He just hoped there wasn't any trouble while they were tripping their heads off. He sure as hell wasn't going to save any hophead, Indian or not. If a man wanted to poison himself, that was his business: He just better not expect Billy Leaps Beeker to come in and save him with the calvary.

Small Eagle stood up. Tsali and Beeker followed his lead.

He walked out of the hogan, still naked. Beeker didn't mind walking into the cooler night air that way, but Tsali automatically covered his crotch with both hands when they got outside. The boy had learned to overcome his shyness around the Black Berets, but the fact that there were women in the village was something he hadn't gotten past yet.

Beeker picked up his briefs and stepped into them, then into his khakis. He continued to dress, pulling on and buttoning his shirt while Tsali and Small Eagle put on their own clothes. Tsali, in a fit of enthusiasm for the traditional ways, had taken to wearing a Coyote Clan loincloth while they were on top of the mesa. It had sounded romantic to the kid, until he realized that it meant he was walking around with half his ass hanging out in front of the women. The loincloth was only about six inches wide and held in place with just a strip of rawhide. That didn't give Tsali a feeling of security.

But the kid wasn't about to admit his embarrassment. He wouldn't pull back from his initial purpose of experiencing this village in all its authenticity. Beeker smiled, and hoped his smile didn't show. He stepped into his boots and then stood, watching Tsali and Small Eagle tie on their moccasins. The little guy was trying so hard, always trying so hard . . .

The three males walked to the fire together. Around it were a group of women. There were more females than males in the village. It had always been the women who maintained the old Indian ways. Beeker remembered the way his grandmother and her cronies used to insist on passing down the legends and the rites to the young girls, assuming, too correctly, that the boys wouldn't pay attention to them.

It was only natural that there would be women who'd flocked to the call of the Native American Crusade here on the Coyote Clan reservation. A few had followed their husbands—men back in the hogan with Rosie. Some were old women who had outlived their mates. And then there was Silver Cloud.

Beeker looked around the gathering as nonchalantly as he could, looking to see if she were there yet. Yes. She was helping one of the wives turn a whole goat over the fire. It had been spitted and rotated over the flames for hours. The outside of the carcass was black with burn, but Beeker knew the meat inside was going to be hot and well cooked. The meat was still sending a steady stream of melted fat down onto the fire.

She was beautiful. She was incredibly beautiful. As Beeker watched her lean over to adjust something on the spit, he saw the way her firm breasts pushed against the dress she was wearing. The back of her skirt lifted up, showing even more of her legs. They were wonderfully proportioned. Not in the way that a white woman's were after a while in a physical fitness class. Silver Cloud's legs were those of an athlete.

He'd found out as much about her as he could. She had made her way through a nearby state university on a rare woman's athletic scholarship. She'd given up a chance to go to the Olympic training camp in Colorado to come here, to the Coyote Clan reservation.

She was half—Coyote Clan. The other half was Navajo. It wasn't a strange mixture in this part of the country. The Navajo were supposed to be the last of the tribes to cross over the now nonexistent land bridge from Asia to the United States. They were the outsiders, the least like the rest of the American Indian tribes.

Silver Cloud's face showed her Navajo blood. It had that strangely Oriental cast to it that the Navajo were famous for. The eyes were narrower, the cheeks higher. It added an element of the exotic to her bearing.

She bent even lower now. Her skirt moved even higher.

Beeker could feel a constraint in his shorts. He was damn glad he wasn't wearing one of the foolish loincloths right now.

*Damn women!* They'd only meant trouble for Beeker. He'd tried marriage twice. Two times it'd been a total failure, and he still sent out two alimony checks a month to prove what a mess those two mistakes had been. Women only want to tame a man, make him some kind of domestic animal—that was what he'd learned from his two mistakes.

They wanted respectability. That meant they didn't like it when a man went out hunting. "What's that horrible smell?" his first wife asked the first time Beeker was leaving their house to get some deer. "Doe piss," he explained simply. "The stags smell it and they come running." The simple, obvious statement had appalled her. She wouldn't let him into their bed for a whole week, and during that week she'd made him shower three times a day. How'd the bitch expect him to get the deer to come his way? Wear goddamned cologne? Everyone knew you wore animal piss on your skin when you went hunting.

This one would be the same, he thought. Oh, she might want him being respectable in an Indian way, but it was always the same—a woman wanting a man to do what she wanted, how she wanted. Silver Cloud'd probably want him to move to some teepee in the desert and eat goat meat for the rest of his life while he sat around in a raw-skin diaper like the one Small Eagle and Tsali had on.

And for what? Why should a man do all that for a woman? Why should he change the way he was? Beeker grabbed a piece of warm pan bread from the nearby stack and chewed on it. He knew why. Goddamn, he knew why, and it made him furious. All because he was sitting here watching a woman's skirt lifting up high enough to show off the back of her thighs.

*Damn.*

Beeker played the stereotype of a stoic Indian for the entire evening meal. Even when Rosie came out with a little too much of a glaze on his eyes, Beeker didn't launch into him the way he ordinarily would have for suspecting that the black man was taking part in a drug-related Coyote Clan activity.

He was trapped in a mixture of anger with himself and a fascination with the manner Silver Cloud had. When Beeker was on the farm in Louisiana, he hardly ever thought about sex. He was just a guy in his house, talking with his friends and doing his work, bringing up his son. Sex wasn't important enough for him to chase after.

It was these times, when he was in close proximity to a woman, that the drive overtook him. He didn't understand how Cowboy and Rosie and the rest of them handled the hassle that came with hunting for sex: the bars, the games, the false promises they all made. It was a farce, he thought. But every so often there'd be a time like this, with someone like Silver Cloud walking around so close—no fake perfumes, not putting on airs, just a woman—and he'd lose it.

There were times with Delilah too. He hated those almost as much. Maybe a little bit less because they happened so often. Delilah made it a contest. She knew how to play Beeker. And maybe that meant he hated having her around even a little bit more than the others, because she had that power and knew it.

The thoughts crowded Beeker's mind. He was furious that they did, keeping his attention away from the other conversations going on. He was furious with his body because it wouldn't stop responding to Silver Cloud. He even snapped at Tsali at one point.

That was inexcusable. "I got to get some sleep," he said, standing up after having eaten a small portion of the goat.

"It's so early," Small Eagle protested. "We're going to sing, the old chants, for the boy. We hoped you'd—"

"Another time," was all that Beeker would say.

He made only the necessary acknowledgments of the other people and then walked away. He went to the guesthouse, where the three of them were staying. He laid down on his pallet and put his arms behind his head, staring at the ceiling, wondering at the problems of men and women. His mind wandered back and forth around the question of talking to Tsali about it. A part of him hoped that Cowboy had taken care of all that. He suspected that Cowboy had given Tsali all the talking to the kid would ever need. But another part of him hoped that the boy hadn't heard a thing from the flier, which meant Beeker should probably take on the responsibility of delivering the talk to him, which he did not want to do.

But he also didn't want to think about Silver Cloud and her high cheekbones and smooth skin either. Because as soon as he did, he started to get aroused again.

There was a movement at the entrance to the hogan. He looked over, careful but not alarmed. He felt safe in this village. He thought it would be Tsali coming to check up on him. But it wasn't. It was Silver Cloud.

Her dress was decorated with beads in a Navajo fashion. The bottom of the skirt was fringed. There was a tight band of bright colored material holding her hair in place. It was richly black. She moved toward him. The pressure in his crotch grew more intense.

"Your boy hoped you'd stay. He wanted you to learn some of the chants to sing to him back home." She delivered her talk without any obvious emotion.

Beeker looked back up at the ceiling. "I know the Cherokee songs. I can sing those to him. I do."

"Yes, but he's interested in all the Indian lore. I think he'd like it if you were able to sing more to him."

"Man's got better things to do than sing to an eighteen-year-old." That was a lie. Beeker loved those moments in the Louisiana forest when the two of them sat down and went through the singsong chants of the Cherokee.

At that moment a booming hymn came from outside, around the campfire. *"Hihihi-hoho-hi."* It was accompanied by the monotone of someone banging on a pot or a drum. It was soon answered with a shriller sound of a different group singing the same sounds.

"The men and women are greeting the full moon," Silver Cloud said. The singing came back as a baritone again. It was a strange sound to a person who grew up with American radio. But something deep inside Beeker knew that it was beautiful—something from his past, even if only his genes knew it.

Silver Cloud began to hum along with the two answering choruses outside. He refused to look at her. But the humming moved closer. She stopped only when she was close enough to him to be heard in a whisper. "The chants of the full moon are a mating chant. Did you know that?"

When her humming started again, the men were singing, *"Hihihi-hoho-hi."*

"You better go find someone to mate with, then," Beeker said. There was sweat gathering in his crotch now, and his armpits. He felt the muscles in his stomach tensing.

"I found one," Silver Cloud whispered.

"No."

Silver Cloud leaned over and kissed his forehead. Her lips felt like red-hot iron on his skin. "It's not easy for an Indian woman to find an Indian man like you."

"I'm just a man." Beeker kept on refusing to look her in the eyes.

"You are. I can see you are." Her hand softly landed on the

fly of his pants. He could feel her fingertips outlining the length of his erection. He closed his eyes.

"Woman, what do you want?"

"A man. Not a drunk. Not a bum. Not someone trying to be whiter than the Anglos. A good, decent, strong Indian man." She leaned farther over and now her lips were on his. Her tongue moved in between his teeth, and he could taste the sweetness of her mouth.

His self-discipline left him. His arms came from the back of his neck and pulled her down on top of his chest. Now those breasts that had tempted his eyes were pressed against him. He could feel the soft and still-firm flesh flattened against his muscles. His palms moved down her back, over the subtle leather of her clothing. It felt as if there were nothing underneath the dress.

In a matter of seconds, they had revolved until he was on top of her, his hard legs spreading hers apart. His erection was stabbing at her, but still sheathed in his pants, it was unable to do anything.

Her hands moved in between their bodies and found the zipper to his khakis. When she met the resistence of his shorts, she simply pulled down on the elastic band.

He pulled away from her and sat up, straddling her hips. He reached down and tore at his slacks, removing them and his boots with efficient motions. He ripped open his shirt and threw it down on a pile with the rest of them. He was still on the pallet, but now he was naked.

He looked down at her, watching the expression on her face. He watched as her hands tentatively came up and touched him. He shifted, and felt her mouth move toward him. He could feel her breath on him. He forced himself to concentrate on that feeling even as he reached down and lifted up her skirt. There was nothing underneath—he'd been right.

He moved away from her, listened when she let out a little groan. She'd made him hot and bothered all day—the sight of her, the feeling of entrapment she'd produced while he studied her. It was time for him to collect for all of it.

He shifted his body again, then knelt between her legs, his knees forcing them far apart, so far that she had to lift up her hips. Her groans came louder.

*"Hihihi-hoho-hi."* Both the men and the women were singing together now. It was the perfect background sound for them.

He loved this part of it—when she started to move her hips. It was his proof that she was in need as much as he was.

"Please," she nearly whimpered.

*"Hihihi-hoho-hi."*

Slowly, he moved into her. Then there was the exquisite feeling as they seemed to mesh together. Finally, he couldn't go inside her anymore.

Now her moans had become a single long chant. It was just as primitive and as melodic to him as the songs outside. Her arms grabbed around his back. Her palms seemed to be caressing each individual muscle he had. He dropped his entire weight on her, sending out a sudden *whoosh* of breath, but not discomforting her so much that her mouth wouldn't reach up and open to his kiss again.

Her moans turned to cries between pain and pleasure. Something close to a grunt greeted each one of his hard thrusts. But she wasn't trying to tell him to stop.

His face contorted in agonized release, and then he collapsed on top of her, his body covered with sweat, his chest heaving with a desperate need for oxygen.

*"Hihihi-hoho-hi . . ."*

# 10

Beeker stepped out of the hogan the next morning. He had to admit he felt a lot better than the day before. It had been a long time since he'd had sex of any kind, and what had happened with Silver Cloud was more than ordinary. He was relaxed, even playful.

He walked over to the fire, where one of the old women was tending a pot of coffee. She smilingly gave him a cup. It was hot and dark, so thick it could have been a syrup. But it tasted good right now.

He scratched his bare chest. It was only six o'clock, but the morning was already warm, and the day would be scorching. Soon he'd have to have his shirt just for the sake of the sun protection it'd give him. But right now the slight breeze that drifted over the mesa was a pleasant relief.

Rosie was back in the hogan snoring away. Silver Cloud had slipped back to her own place before the chanting had finished. Beeker had been sound asleep by the time the others had come in. Still, Tsali was up and about already. He was wondering where the boy was.

He heard it before he saw it. It was a series of *whomp* sounds from behind the circle of hogans in the village. Beeker carried his coffee cup to see what was going on.

Tsali and Small Eagle were standing about two hundred feet from a target. They were using bows to send arrows toward the bull's-eye. When Beeker scowled, it wasn't because of the memory of Tsali's use of bow and arrow to take out the men back at the Louisiana farm. It was because of the type of equipment the boy was using.

"So that's your idea of *traditional*?" Beeker said loudly.

Tsali froze.

Small Eagle looked back, slightly puzzled. "What's wrong?"

Beeker walked over to the two of them and lifted up the complicated piece of machinery Small Eagle was holding. "A compound bow? What's wrong with a good old-fashioned recurve? What do you need all these pulleys and angles and shit for?"

"A compound bow lets a small man or a boy get all the power of a seventy-pound draw," Small Eagle said. "I'm not sure I would have known just how well it could work if it wasn't for your son."

"My son?" Beeker was incredulous. All of a sudden he realized that Tsali was still frozen in his position, facing away from the two men's conversation. He reached over and pulled the bow out of Tsali's hand and examined it. "Is this *yours*?"

Tsali nodded slowly.

"Where did you get it?"

Tsali finally turned around and his hands flashed.

"I should have known. Cowboy! Your present from San Francisco! Guy gets you all involved in computers, and then, next thing I know, he's messing you up with foolish bows!"

Tsali started to argue. Small Eagle looked on, able to follow the conversation only by watching the boy's facial expressions and by listening to Beeker's half of the conversation. For a kid who couldn't talk, he obviously was able to give his father a lot of good arguments.

"I know, I know, you can't hold back a recurve bow with a seventy-pound draw for more than a minute, tops. But you can use a forty-pound draw! That's good enough for the rabbit hunting you do at home. You can handle a forty-pound draw easy."

Small Eagle knew perfectly well what they were talking about. The draw of a bow is the measure of the pressure it takes to retract it. A forty-pound draw took forty pounds of pressure; a seventy-pound draw took seventy pounds of effort.

But the strength necessary to pull back the string was nothing compared to the exertion a hunter had to use to keep it in place. All but the strongest men started to shake if they had to hold back a seventy-pound draw for very long. The shaking ruined their chances for accuracy, especially at a long distance.

But a kid like Tsali, who was well trained on a small draw, could take a compound bow and only have to use the same power to get the awesome force and accuracy of a much larger draw.

It was achieved by a series of pulleys at the top and bottom of the bow. Rather than having the string simply connected to the two tips, it wound through the pulleys and each one increased the pressure of the release without affecting the pressure needed for the withdrawal.

It was simple science, added to one of man's most simple weapons.

Beeker was suddenly quiet. Small Eagle looked at him with puzzlement. "What is it? What did the boy say?" Something had struck Beeker with a powerful blow.

"He said he wasn't always going to be hunting rabbits."

Small Eagle watched a change in Beeker's expression. The tall half-breed Cherokee finally nodded to his son.

"Okay, then let's do it right."

Beeker moved behind Tsali and coached his son while the young man continued to shoot his blunt-tipped arrows at the target.

Small Eagle walked through the motions of keeping pace with Tsali's target practice, but he felt that something more than recreational shooting was going on between father and son. He learned just what in a short time.

"See that target you're using?" Beeker asked. Tsali nodded agreement. Beeker took one of the blunt-tipped practice arrows and reached into the side pocket of the quiver Tsali was using. He handled the contents very carefully. Soon he pulled out the broadhead attachments. He took one and screwed it onto the tip. Then he took another of the razor-sharp attachments and put it on the broadhead. The result was an aluminum shaft, aerodynamically designed, with four sharp edges. "Go ahead—that target has about the consistency of a man's belly. Shoot it."

Tsali pulled back the bow and let his arrow fly through the air. *Whomp*. Beeker beckoned to Tsali to follow him to the target. When they got there, they could see that the arrow had totally penetrated the straw figure. Only the end was still inside, barely holding the shaft to the structure.

"That's what you can do with a seventy-pound draw on an arrow, recurve or compound. Don't you ever forget what it can do."

Tsali solemnly nodded his promise.

Small Eagle had to again wonder why that normal-sounding exchange hadn't been the simple statement he would have usually accepted it as. Then it came to him: If he had heard a father give that small lecture at another time, it would have been an admonition to be careful, a warning that a weapon is dangerous. But Billy Leaps Beeker hadn't done that. He hadn't warned his son that the compound bow was risky; he had pointed out its utility. It wasn't something that Tsali should be uncertain about; it was something he should control.

Small Eagle gained a great deal of respect for both father and son. These were warriors, real warriors. They were learning, and they were preparing in the same essential manner that their forefathers had, decades ago. They were men he wanted to have on his side.

"Man, space-age bows and arrows. What will they think of next?" Rosie was getting his chance to practice on the compound bows later in the morning. "Who'd ever think that a black man from Newark would end up shooting these things."

Whoever would have doubted it would have been surprised. Rosie had learned to shoot a bow and arrow on the farm in Louisiana. It had been an easy way to spend a few hours with Tsali on a hot day. He was close to being a marksman.

One after another the men would walk up to the line, take their aim, then let their arrows fly. "Too bad," Rosie said, "we're always stuck using messy guns and bullets."

"Who knows," Small Eagle said as he took his mark and prepared to try to match Rosie's near bull's-eye. "You know, I went to Las Vegas to this Indian meeting the other week, and there was this T-shirt with 'What if . . .' written on it below a picture of one of these. Man, if my ancestors had these things, your cavalry wouldn't have had a chance."

"My cavalry!" Rosie scoffed. "Those guys had my great-grandmother in chains back on the plantation. Don't try to pin that one on me."

Small Eagle's bow twanged, sending his arrow flying across the target area. It landed perfectly in the middle of the eye. He stood back and smiled with satisfaction.

Rosie whistled with appreciation. "And don't pin one of *those* fuckers on me either."

Someone called out. All four males turned and saw Silver Cloud coming toward them. Beeker tried not to look into her eyes. He didn't want her to see his attraction to her, and he didn't want Tsali to see it either.

She walked up to them with an envelope in her hand. "For you." Beeker suddenly was startled to realize she was talking to him. He took it from her.

"Cowboy," was all he said. He opened the flap and pulled out a letter. "Trouble."

"Don't you love the way he just goes on and on. It lets you know why he and Tsali get on so well," Rosie complained.

Tsali smiled at the joke.

Beeker shoved the letter into his pocket. "It's time we went and had a talk about things. We've got plans to make."

Small Eagle looked at him for a while. "We just want to hold the mesa. That's all the Crusade people want. My father and the council just want to get their court case taken care of. They've already won; now they want to collect."

"Seems like there are a lot of people who are going to activate you a little bit more than that. A lot of people."

Small Eagle had called a couple of the other men to join them. There were seven men around the circle, including Beeker, Rosie, and Tsali. And there was Silver Cloud. Beeker looked at her with a questioning expression.

"Don't try to tell me I don't belong here, Mr. Beeker. I do. I've got more to do with the Coyote Clan than you."

Beeker checked it out with Small Eagle. The lack of response from the leader of the Native American Crusade indicated he would back her up.

"Okay. Our information tells us that you are all in for a lot more trouble. A lot more. What's happened so far is just a setup. We've seen it before. A group comes in and causes things to happen. It gets people used to a little touch of violence, makes them nervous, on edge, jumpy. Things are happening, but no one knows just what they are.

"It gives them a cover to do much more. Someone's pulling together a group of men who are going to do something. It's all we got right now. But that something is going to affect you, I know that.

"What do you know about Nevari?" Beeker asked.

He was surprised when Silver Cloud answered: "It's a large corporation, no doubt about it. But it's had hard times in other parts of the world. It's been kicked out of a couple of countries that didn't like the way they did business. But they have enough oil and coal and other things going on in this area that they saved themselves. That's why everyone always talks about them being the ones who'll be hit hardest by the court decisions.

"They not only stand to lose the most in every way; they also stand to lose almost all of what they have left."

She shrugged. "Besides that, they're a big company. They act like it. They have this hotshot president—"

"Adamson." Beeker looked at the pieces of paper in his hand.

"Yes, Adamson," Silver Cloud continued. "He's a big booster for the region. The usual public relations–minded executive. They pay regular; they are the favorites of the local politicians. They own a lot of things, contribute to a lot of charities."

"But their back's against the wall?" Beeker said.

"Yes." Small Eagle joined the conversation. "They hired lawyers to fight the case—they didn't leave it to the state or federal authorities; they brought in their own people. They claimed they'd be ruined."

"These corporations are like sleeping bears," Silver Cloud said. "You think they're all nice and calm and benevolent, but then you wake them up, and they'll show you what they're made of."

"I think Nevari's going to do just that," Beeker said.

"Well, we'll just get the federal authorities to stop them. Take them to court. We'll alert our lawyers—"

Beeker interrupted Silver Cloud: "I don't think you understand. The way it looks, by the time they're finished, there might not be any of you left to hire lawyers. I don't think they're going to be that nice about the whole thing."

He turned to Rosie. "They got the sheriff here in their pocket. Complete sellout, I bet. We've heard about that before. Seems the sheriff's got orders to hire a special contingency force for some reason. He's going to be hiring down in Mesa City, I bet.

"No one's really seen you. There haven't been any people but the Coyote Clan up here since Tsali and I joined them, and most of the time you were back in Mesa City you were at the motel or in the library and you were dressed pretty city-like. I bet no one would recognize you if you were to start hanging around in some of the bars in Mesa City, whatever bars the police and the sheriff deputies like to go to."

"You want me to get myself recruited?" Rosie said.

"You got it," Beeker answered.

"And us?" Small Eagle asked. "What do you think we're going to do?"

"I think if you're smart, you and your men are going to spend a lot of time target shooting with some damn good rifles. I think this mesa may be in for another last stand. Maybe you better be damn well prepared to defend it as well as your ancestors did."

# 11

It doesn't matter if it was a small place like Mesa City or a great metropolis like New York. Every city has at least one bar where the peacekeepers hang out.

Rosie loved that word: *peacekeepers*.

He especially loved it when it was applied to a joint like Stoney's Bar and Grill. He was sure this was the least peaceful bar in Mesa County. Whenever a place got the privilege of being the cop joint, the word spread. The word didn't only bring in people to have a good time when they were off duty, it didn't just tell them where they'd be welcome—it always assured the place that it would never have to worry about any kind of bust again.

But bars like Stoney's were always the least lawful in any city. They were the ones where you could buy dope, 'cause the off-duty cops had to have a place to get high. When you bought dope at Stoney's, you didn't have to worry about being busted, since the person doing the selling would have been the narc who'd have pinched you anywhere else.

Male cops gotta have a piece of ass when they want that too, Rosie thought. There were always lots of prossies working in a joint like this. Course, he mused as he sipped on his beer, with all the lady police nowadays it was only a matter of time before they had to import some fancy men for them. Equal opportunity knows no limits.

But the drugs and the sex were minor, very minor things at Stoney's. Because what really went on when the peacekeepers got off duty was not peaceful. It was violent as hell. He'd counted three fistfights in less than an hour. In fact, while he was working on his first draft beer, Rosie had to slide to one side while an off-duty bluecoat went flying over the bar and smashed his head on the ledge behind it. He'd been hit by someone who claimed to be the head of the local state police barracks.

Why? Rosie wondered. Probably because all these men and women spent their whole day dealing with physical attacks that they weren't supposed to respond to. They were constantly breaking up domestic fights—the largest number of police calls in any municipality in the United States—or they were dealing with the sorry cases they could never get a handle on. There'd be the heroin pushers who would have fancy shyster lawyers to get them off. There'd be the pimps who hurt their girls and then the girls wouldn't dare to testify. Worst of all, there'd be the child-abuse calls—the times when a cop would go into a house and see a fresh bruise on a kid's bottom that looked just like the decoration on the family waffle iron. But the social workers would say it couldn't be. The parents didn't fit some magical "profile," so they must be telling the truth—the kid fell down the stairs, and the marks were only coincidentally symmetrical.

That must be the worst for a good cop, Rosie thought.

Rosie hated that. Rosie hated to think what he'd do if he came across that. He wouldn't like to know what he'd be like if he got that angry.

He saw a couple of pool players, obviously off-duty bluecoats, off in the corner. They were arguing over some stupid rule. Rosie quickly checked out his position as first one, then the other of the players lifted their sticks. Rosie knew all too well that while a pool stick would certainly break the first time it was used to deliver a good blow, that one good blow would hurt like hell. He did not want to be the recipient.

He knew he was cool—there was plenty of space to either side. He'd just keep an eye on the threatening altercation in case it flared up. He relaxed a bit when the men seemed to go back to their game. He sipped his beer.

Rosie thought some more about cops. Yeah, he believed they worked under horrible pressures, and he knew that some of them broke. He also knew that some of them could be mean sons of bitches. He'd met more than his share growing up in Newark. The racist assholes who thought that it was open season on any black kid old enough to walk.

The hotshots who thought that beating up a woman while they were in uniform was just one of the perks of the job.

They were bad, evil.

But the worst—the ones who were the scum of any force, who fed on the good ones in the uniforms as well as on the civilians—were terrible. The ones who took payoffs. The ones who used their positions to help politicians. The ones who were for sale.

Rosie called for another beer. Those, he knew, were the ones he was waiting for. He was bait for them tonight. He was sitting there waiting to spot one.

The door to Stoney's opened just as Rosie paid for his new draft. He looked to see who'd walked in and immediately realized that he wasn't going to get just one; he was going to be blessed with a table full.

They were all Mesa County sheriff deputies. That, he knew,

was already one down on them. The cops in Mesa City were pretty decent. They were responsible only for the city's borders. They got the traffic stuff for this burg, all forty thousand people, and they had a city just large enough to make them have to deal with all the ugly shit of urban life.

They had a nice clean little civic government, and they got all kinds of awards from the state government. Some of the plaques were hanging on the wall right here at Stoney's.

But the Mesa County sheriff had a lot more going his way. His jurisdiction spread over hundreds of square miles. It was a land area larger than some states back East. There was no other city besides Mesa City, the county seat, that had its own police force. The deputies were responsible for the towns, for all the regular highways, for murder investigations, and for everything that happened on the Coyote Clan reservation as well. Or they had been until the court case came up. The case meant that the local authorities had no more role in peacekeeping on the reservation.

The reservation, according to the new definition, included every square inch of Mesa County. That table full of deputies was going to be a table full of unemployed men because of the courts.

Rosie knew just how bad the Mesa County deputies were when he saw the expressions of contempt that came over two state troopers sitting near him at the bar. They would have gladly spit at the five men who claimed the round table on the other side of the room. They made no move to hide that feeling. But soon they went back to their beers. They only had to worry about the major state highways. What vermin like the deputies did was no concern of theirs.

Or maybe they had been told not to make it their concern. Rosie studied the troopers and thought that must be just what was happening. It was that same expression of loathing he'd seen on cops' faces when they had some ironclad bust to make, and the higher-ups told them to back off. They knew something was wrong, but their hands were tied.

You usually only got that with drugs or corruption of some major sort. But that same process seemed to be happening right now, right here in Mesa County.

It was getting late. The shifts had changed about two hours ago for the city police. Most of the customers had just come in to blow off some steam. The pool players went home happy, never having gotten around to breaking those cues over each other's heads. One by one, couple by couple, Stoney's emptied out.

The state troopers left as soon as they had finished their beer. Whether it was normal timing for them or whether the Mesa County deputies had made the place stink, Rosie wasn't sure. He was just pleased that the thinned-out crowd was going to make things easier.

The five men were enjoying their second pitcher of beer. They were the kind of uniformed men who invited the most vicious hatred in anyone who had to deal with them. Rosie tried to study them carefully to see if there was any redeeming feature about any one of them. There wasn't.

They were all overweight. Two of them had guts that hung so far over their belts that Rosie bet it'd been years since they'd seen their peckers. They talked with that loud bravado of a man who isn't satisfied that he's a man and needs public assurance that other people see him as something hot, something macho.

Rosie knew that these were the kinds who did everything wrong. And it made them the right ones for him. He wished that one of them had been black or at least noticeably Hispanic. Then he could at least try to pull some soul brother shit on him. But they all seemed Anglo. Rosie wondered for a while if he was the right one to pull this assignment. It didn't appear as though the Mesa County Sheriff's Department was going to be a major practitioner of affirmative action.

One of the men stood up to bring the pitcher back to the bar for a refill. He was one of the two with the biggest gut. They all seemed to look so much alike to Rosie that the size of their stomachs was the only real way he could distinguish them. They all had on tinted sunglasses, the same dull brown uniforms, the same thinning hair, tanned faces, and uniform hats.

The one guy stood beside Rosie. He already had a glow on from his beer. Rosie had watched him as he'd guzzled twice as much from the pitcher as the rest of them.

"You new in town?" the deputy asked while he waited for the bartender.

"Sure am," Rosie replied. He was going to have to fake a lot of things in this conversation, that was for sure. Friendliness might be the easiest of all of them. "How'd you ever find Stoney's?"

Rosie wondered if the question was argumentative. Was the man really saying, *What's a nigger doing here?* No, he was just shooting the shit. "Friends from Bakersfield told me about it."

"You from there?"

"Sure am." Smile, Rosie, smile, he commanded himself.

"Fine music from Bakersfield. Fine music. I think it's the best country and western music in the nation. That Nashville shit's all gone pop, all gone to plastic, if you ask me. I think Bakersfield's the future."

Bakersfield, California, is the future? Then I'm packing it in for Nigeria, Rosie thought. But he smiled. He'd pulled Bakersfield out of his hat, just a California city not too far away that would make sense. A place where a cop might have told him about Stoney's if he'd asked. He'd forgotten that it really was a major center for recording and producing country music.

"But a friend told you about our little place here? Stoney's?" The deputy had given the empty pitcher over to the bartender.

"Yeah." *Be careful, now, this has to work.* "A guy I was in the MPs with. In 'Nam. He and I are tight. He knew I was drifting down this way. Thought I might like some places to go, you know, where I'd feel comfortable. He's a cop down there."

"Oh." The beer-bellied man stood up and smiled. "You're a cop?"

"No, no, I was in the MPs. I'm just a plain civilian now."

"That's strange," the deputy said, "I thought that most of you guys didn't find it easy. You know, going to a straight job. Besides, you all had that training; you could just move into a force, get some veterans' points, all that."

The pitcher was delivered, and one of the other deputies yelled over and complained about the time it was taking to move it from the bar to the table.

"Well, let's say I didn't leave the Army with the kind of record that makes for quick employment in the police."

"But you left with the kind of record that your friend, the cop, still thinks you're okay?"

"You sort of got it. You know, there are lots of ways to make the service mad at you. Lots of ways to keep from getting hired with all the rules and regulations. They're pretty unforgiving of a guy, no matter what he did, no matter how long ago he did it."

"Matt, get your lard ass over here with our beer!" the voice griped again.

"Just drifting?"

"For a while. I pick up some things to do every now and then."

"I bet you do." Lardass Matt studied Rosie for a minute. "Why don't you come on over and join us for a while. Might be something coming up for you right here."

"Why, I'd be glad to." *Sucker.*

Rosie sure as hell didn't have to fake any references to get this job. As a matter of fact, as he took in the rest of the crew in the camp, he figured that anyone who had any real credentials would have been automatically disqualified.

This was one hell of a dangerous crew. Any way you looked at it, this was a bunch of explosions waiting to go off.

They were in an abandoned mining camp about ten miles from Mesa City. There wasn't another structure or man-made landmark to be seen. There were just two long barracks-like buildings. But that was the end of any military comparison.

There was the full number of men here that Cowboy had predicted. Fifty of them. They were every color, every size, every shape. The only thing they had in common was that they were all ready to blow.

One by one, Rosie would have taken any of them seriously. He knew their type. They were the kind of men who never stay in one place long enough to become an organized crime force. They didn't have the drive or the self-discipline or the interest or the *something* that would have made them regular criminals.

But there certainly were criminals in the group. Probably every one of them had committed a felony. Rosie was sure of that. But they were men who wandered the country looking for some excitement, looking for something to divert them. Rosie figured their usual diversions were stuff like rape, armed robbery, maybe a little murder now and then.

They fell into groups. There were, as always, the veterans—those scarred men from Vietnam who'd never come back to the civilized. They'd tasted blood and they wanted more. But they didn't have a Billy Leaps Beeker to give their urges and their needs any sense. They just had the lust.

Rosie decided to play it as if he were one of them. He'd teamed up with another black man, Washington Jones, who was the most authentic in the group. Washington had a certain look about him, one that spoke of both vacantness and potential violence at the same time.

"Bro, these are some stupid motherfuckers," Washington had said to him the morning Rosie arrived. "These assholes don't want to shoot no guns in the morning; they don't want to smoke no weed. What they expect to *do* in the morning?" Washington Jones obviously found this a pressing question.

"Hey, man, I don't know what they are. Why don't you tell me?"

"Man, I'll tell you anything, you smoke some dope with me. Man, I shouldn't have to do weed all by myself."

"You're on."

Washington had given him the layout fast and furious, and undeniably accurately. There were four other vets in the camp. "They okay," Washington announced as he sucked in the marijuana at eight o'clock in the morning.

And Rosie was all right himself, Washington soon decided. The black man picked up Rosie's gear and led him into the first barracks. Most of the men were still in bed. "This is the blood corner," Washington proudly announced.

Over a group of five cots hung a huge piece of black velvet cloth. On it was sewn a silver-like portrait of a skull.

Washington pointed to Rosie's earring and laughed. "You *deserve* to sleep under my banner."

With that, he dropped Rosie's duffel bag on a sleeping body on the cot nearest the group of five. "What the fuck!" yelled a voice in a decidedly southern accent. The body jumped out of the cot dressed only in a pair of jockey shorts. Its fists were lifted up, ready to do battle. Rosie knew instinctively that this man would have taken out any other person besides Washington Jones. But as soon as the guy saw who it was, the hands went down.

"We taking your cot, white trash. You go away—find yourself a place with the other crackers. We got a blood bro needs this one."

The man Washington was talking to was no small person. This wasn't someone who would normally walk away from a demeaning encounter like this. But even while he scowled, the man began to pack up his things.

"Come on, bro, leave your stuff." Washington Jones flashed his crazy eyes and nodded toward the door.

Rosie followed Jones, studying his body from the rear. Washington and he were about the same size, and they were in about the same shape as well, with shoulders wider than they should be on any normal man. The arms were powerfully huge. Washington had on a strapped T-shirt, his black skin pulled tight over big knots of hard flesh.

Rosie had seen his type countless times. They were all crazy. They were crazy in Vietnam. They were the ones who would sense every possible weakness in a commander of any rank and then play it. They were the ones who could end up humiliating an NCO, giving some kind of caustic comeback at every moment and then daring the other man to enforce an order with physical action—action that was the only way to subdue them and certain to end up in their favor.

In prison, this was the kind of man who terrorized the cellblock. When he was a kid, Washington Jones undoubtedly was the one who stole the other kids' lunch money and used it to buy himself a soda.

This was exactly the kind of man who the Marine Corps loved to get its hands on. He was made to be a drill instructor. He was *born* to be one. Give him that structure, place the slightest bit of rules upon him in return for the promise that he could do so very much more, legally, and you had the makings of a fine sadist. A man who could derive great pleasure from the suffering of eighteen-year-olds. The kind of man who would exult in the humiliation of every single grunt who walked through the gates.

But leave him alone, give him some smoke, too much to drink? You had an animal on the loose.

Roosevelt Boone looked at Washington Jones and immediately realized something. They were going to have to have a fight soon, and Rosie was going to have to win. Or else Rosie would end up having to kill this man. There was no middle ground. There was no choice. Washington Jones would respect only one thing: brute strength greater than his own. Rosie was going to have to show it to him.

They walked to the mess tent. Rosie followed Washington Jones down the chow line, and each of them piled their metal plates high with scrambled eggs, bacon, toast. They balanced glasses of milk and orange juice on the trays, then made their way toward an empty table sheltered from the sun by a tarp above. The sides of the tent were open to the slight breeze. It was much too hot in this part of Nevada to stay in any kind of enclosed space.

"What's the line here?" Rosie asked, working hard to make sure his questions came out easily and without any pressure behind them.

"Well, bro, we got to go through some tests, see. Show 'em we know how to use a gun, know how to fight a man, those martial arts things, you know? Then we got some indoctrination. Just like 'Nam. It's bullshit, but we got to make the man happy.

"We're going to move real soon, I hear. No time to bother with all the marching in formation shit. Just as well." Washington Jones obviously didn't care for that part of training. "We're going to bust some heads real good and in our own way." That idea brought a smile back to his face.

"Who're we doing this for?" Rosie asked, taking a bite of eggs.

"Who gives a shit?" Jones replied. "I mean, a man pays you, tells you you can't get in any trouble with the law—"

"How do we know that?" Rosie was careful to use a tone of voice that dripped with contempt for any promises from authorities. Men like Washington Jones, men like the person Rosie was supposed to be, would expect that cynicism.

"Yeah, I know, I know." Washington Jones shook his head with understanding. "Can't really trust 'em. I know that. But you look around. You a smart boy—you look around and see things. There's *signs*, if you know how to read them. Talk to me tonight, bro. Tell me if you haven't seen the *signs*."

Their first stop was the marksmanship test. Rosie sometimes faked it, purposely missing enough scores so he wouldn't stand out. But this time it seemed different. He thought he should make a very positive impression.

He stood in line waiting his turn. He kept playing with Washington Jones's tease that he should look for signs. They might as well have been on a billboard.

The marksman test was a walk-through. All they wanted to know was if a man knew how to use a rifle. They were so confident of their selections that the leaders were taking the easy way out: they were distributing the arms they expected the men to use to confirm the guys would know what they were for.

As each man stepped up to the line, he was handed a Mini-14 and a forty-round magazine of 5.56 NATO rounds. The rifles and the ammunition came from clearly marked wooden crates, which announced not only the manufacturer—Ruger—but also the purchaser. The Mesa County sheriff's office. Both names were hand-stenciled on the wood.

Rosie knew the gun well. It could be bought in a lot of

hunting supply stores. But then the ammunition would be marked as .233 caliber. This stuff was gotten through official channels. Someone was sure enough about his ability to win a fight that he wasn't worried about any other authorities making investigations. The clearly marked military ammunition was available to law enforcement offices around the country.

The Mini-14 was their favorite rifle. Those forty-round magazines could shoot off as fast as the human finger could pull the trigger. The semiautomatic weapon was a deadly alternative to the machine guns denied to most big-city police departments.

Rosie took his gun, which still smelled of fresh grease. He looked at the redneck deputy and smiled. It was one of the ones who had been drinking beer with Lardass Matt at Stoney's. The deputy remembered him and returned the greeting.

Rosie put one foot on the mark and sighted the Mini-14. "Only got to show me you know what it's about," the deputy began to say. But Rosie had already begun pulling the trigger of the rifle with incredible speed. All forty rounds burst over the target area and embedded themselves in the paper target that had been stapled to a thick wooden backup.

Only when they had all been fired did Rosie lower his gun.

"Hotshot, huh?" the deputy said. Then he walked the length of the target range and picked the paper off the backup. He looked back at Rosie from the distance; Rosie sensed his plan had worked. There was a grudging respect in the man's expression. The deputy walked back carrying the piece of paper in his hand. He showed it to Rosie. Only two of the small holes were outside the bull's-eye.

"Hell," Rosie said, "Missed *two*. You still want me?"

The deputy nodded, acknowledging Rosie's joke with a more somber smirk now. "I think you'll do. I think we might even want you on a special team."

"That's good news, man, real good news." Rosie kept his gun and grabbed some more magazines from the ammunition box, then walked over to the place where Washington Jones was waiting for him.

"You trying to show me up?" Jones asked. It wasn't a friendly gesture.

Rosie was puzzled. Washington had obviously passed, and had a rifle in his hand. Rosie hadn't even noticed what Washington Jones had scored on his test.

"I'm the bad nigger in this camp, bro," Jones said. "I don't need no competition from you."

The big black man turned away and stormed over to the physical fitness area. Rosie understood. A dopehead like Jones could change on a man in a matter of minutes, seconds. He was the star, in his own hopped-up head. Anyone who took the limelight from him was danger. Rosie had gotten the attention he wanted from the boss men, but he'd gotten some undesired attention as well.

That's the way it goes, Rosie thought. You stand up, and you get shot. Except anyone expecting to shoot Roosevelt Boone had better remember that he had a Mini-14 in his own hand too.

Rosie walked slowly over to the physical tests. He could see that Washington Jones wasn't moving moderately. The black man had surged across the dusty flat area and was already stripping off his T-shirt before Rosie had caught up with him. Rosie understood that Jones needed a victory.

It was one of the things that made a man like Jones so dangerous. He was the kind of man who would get a little cutting remark from his lady at home and then, to make up for it, he'd have to go out and rape the first defenseless woman he found. It was his own special way of evening the balance of power. Or else, when he was younger and his big brother had beaten him up, he'd take a handgun and go shoot the eyes out of the man who owned the corner store. His own humiliations, no matter how slight, no matter how meaningless they'd look to an outsider, could only be compensated for by some greater violent act performed on someone else. It was the only way that a person like Jones could get back.

Now, the wrestling arena was going to give him a chance to fight someone. He was fuming, his chest heaving with anticipation and his fists curled into tight weapons. He wanted to taste blood to make up for the idea that another black man could have outdone him on the shooting range.

Rosie was torn. He could either make this the time and place he put Washington Jones in his place. Or else he could let the man release a little steam, let go of a little pressure, and they could go back to being blood buddies again. There was a lot of benefit to either decision.

Someone else made his mind up for him. The deputy from the shooting range was accompanying another man over to the physical fitness section. The man was the boss. Rosie knew it immediately. A glance at his name tag proved him right. The deputy was pointing out Rosie to the sheriff right now. The star boy of the target range was someone to watch, and Sheriff Mike Passak wanted to do just that.

Rosie whistled some more. *Be all that you can be . . .*

He checked out his options. The tests were stupid. Just like the target range, the deputies just wanted to make sure they had paid for adequate meat to send into their fight, whatever it might be. If you shot off your rounds at the range and proved you knew how to hold and fire a rifle, you got your weapon.

Now, you went one-on-one with another guy, proved you could take a couple of painful punches without crying, knew how to grapple with a guy, and then you went on. There was a slight obstacle course, one so easy that Billy Leaps would have spit on it, but it would serve its purpose. It just proved you could run a certain distance, do a certain number of push-ups, and then climb over some things. Then you got your equipment. Rosie could see that at the end of the course.

To go along with your Mini-14, you got a handgun—he couldn't tell what kind. You got a knife with a sheath that fit on your belt. A couple of grenades and a few pieces of paper, probably identification. They were loading up these men with a lot of hardware, that was for sure.

Rosie turned back and looked at Sheriff Passak. The man was like the deputies, physically. He had a pot, the same brown uniform and uniform hat, the same dark glasses. He was trying to hide his intentions, but Rosie knew he was looking his way. It was his chance to make himself known.

The two men in the center of the dozen men waiting their turn were scuffling on the dusty ground. They were street fighters, dirty fighters going after eyes and balls with hands and feet.

They could go at it for an hour, Rosie bet. They would be terrible mothers to meet in a dark alley, but they would also be easy marks for Rosie. They were totally undisciplined. If a trained fighter moved on them, they wouldn't have known what had happened.

He studied them even more carefully. They were both Hispanic. Probably petty thieves on the run from the law in Los Angeles or Phoenix, they'd happened on an opportunity here in Nevada. Or else they could have been illegal immigrants, ready to earn their money any way they could without a green card.

As they rolled over the ground, tossing up small clouds of dust, Rosie could see they were marked with amateur tattoos up and down their arms and even on their chests and bellies. They were the type of tattoos you only got in one of two places: the barrios of Southern California or Arizona or the prison cells of any one of fifty states.

Forget the noble image of poor Mexicans doing what they had to for a buck. These guys were the real thing, real hard cases.

Out of the corner of his eye Rosie saw the sheriff nudge the deputy with his elbow. The underling put a silver whistle to his lips and blew hard. The signal was to end the fight. Those Chicanos were having too good a time though. Wild young males brought up in the barrio still hadn't found a better way to pass the day than to fight with one another.

A couple of other deputies had to move in and pry them apart. It took two of the uniformed men to hold each of the Chicanos, who were furious. They growled at one another across the small clearing, vowing and swearing in Spanish.

Then, suddenly realizing the fun was over, they both relaxed. They were released and started to smile at each other. Their smiles revealed gaps where teeth used to be. They clasped each other on the shoulder, then moved and retrieved their shirts and started to walk to the next station. They were back to being best friends.

Rosie had a perfectly good idea why the sheriff had ended the fight. It wasn't simply in order to save the energy of a couple of recruits. Passak was just interested in getting the next act onstage as soon as possible.

Washington Jones jumped ahead of whoever was next and stood in the circle. "Come on, chumps, I need some action," he yelled at the men. Rosie watched them and saw most take an unconscious step backward. Jones had made his reputation early in this group. No one was particularly anxious to challenge him.

The sheriff's head moved more toward Rosie. He was waiting. Rosie decided not to keep the man in suspense.

"You got it, bro," Rosie announced and moved through the

small crowd to stand in front of Jones. He handed his rifle to a bystander, then pulled off his shirt and tossed it aside.

Jones scowled. "You be careful. You may be blood, but you still pussy compared to Washington Jones. You should be real careful."

"Pussy?" Rosie smiled. "This ass's been in more stockades than you can count, and more'n enough jails. Ain't never been any man's pussy though. Can you say that? Huh, Jones? Bet you were a pretty boy when you got behind the man's bars the first time."

Jones's shock was so great that he dropped his hands. They'd been held up and out in preparation for a fight. He'd been bent over, already beginning to turn and weave. But the idea that any man would dare to make that accusation was more than he could bear.

"I thought you was a friend," Jones said, honest hurt in his voice.

"I'll prove what a friend I am, bro. When I finish beating your ass, I won't kill you. How's that for friendship?"

The cluster of men laughed out loud. They'd been tense at first, wondering how this new black man was going to do with Jones. Now that they saw what he was made of, that he dared to challenge Jones this way, they were hopeful that maybe he could really beat the intimidating man.

Jones resumed his fighting stance. His eyes were alight again with insane rage. Rosie thought over the situation. His usual approach would have been quick, effective, and to the point. He'd just move in and take the other black man out. But he had an audience and he wanted to play to it. He was out to make an impression, not just win the fight.

When he'd been in training with the Rangers, Rosie had learned all the funny things that went with the martial arts. They weren't very impressive when a man was going up against an enemy who wasn't interested in theatrics. But they sure looked good when you were getting points for delivery. Rosie understood that the sheriff and his men—all those beer-bellied deputies with their macho image dependent on guns and the perception of their authority—really weren't used to hand-to-hand combat. They'd use a blackjack or a billy club in a fight, or else they'd make sure they could handle any altercation with their firearms.

They were the ones who packed theaters when they showed Oriental films of the Ninja or the masters of karate, not because they understood the perfection that some of the actors displayed, but because the men seemed to be practicing magic more than anything else.

Show time, Rosie told himself.

*"Hiiii-yyaaahhh!"*

Washington Jones was stunned. His face showed it immediately. What was this nigger doing with all those funny noises? Rosie was actually putting himself through one of the loudest, but most authentic, displays of Chinese goju, the purest form of judo. His hands were held up in traditional form, the palms straight out, ready to be used as fighting tools as lethal as any metal bludgeon.

Jones regained himself and started to move in a circular flow to test out this strange stuff he was seeing. Rosie hotdogged it a bit more. *"Yyyaaahh-ha!"* He jumped in the air and landed in a place perfect to face Jones. The other black man lunged forward, ready to land a punch that should have knocked Rosie out. But when he swung, there was only air.

Jones had no choice but to follow through, all the way till his feet fell out from underneath him. He flew through the air and landed with his body insisting on a continued forward motion. He jumped up, confused and with a noseful of dust.

Rosie thought that had all been impressive enough.

*"Sayaaaanoooorah!"* No one got his joke. They were all too busy being impressed by the way Rosie leaped through the air feet-first and slammed his heels into Jones's chest, knocking every bit of air out of the man's lungs. Jones collapsed on the ground, gasping for breath.

But Jones was really inhumanly strong. No one else would have been able to struggle to his sitting position. He was trying hard to get back his composure. He shook his head quickly, as though it could allow him to make sense of what was going on.

Rosie was disgusted with himself. The sound effects might have been good acting, but that shouldn't have allowed Jones to recover so quickly. Forget the frosting, Rosie went for the cake. His foot, heavily booted with a steel toe, lashed out and caught Jones right below the ribs. There was a loud, sharp *crack!* At least a couple of Jones's ribs were broken.

Jones opened his mouth to yell, but all that came out was a weak whimper. Everyone else seemed to freak, thinking he was going to die. But Rosie knew the broken ribs weren't lethal. So he just stood back and crossed his arms over his chest.

The deputy's whistle sounded shrilly. "Medic!" some voice called out. Jones lost consciousness and fell back onto the ground.

Rosie walked over to the sheriff. He was alone now—his aide had evidently been the one rushing for a doctor.

"So, boss, I got that special assignment your boy hinted at?"

There was no way to see through the reflecting surface of the sheriff's glasses. But Rosie knew there was also no way he wasn't being studied. "Got some things a man like you might be useful for."

"Got double pay attached to it?" Rosie asked.

"Pretty pushy. You ain't starving on the wages you're getting."

"No, not starving, but there's always some good reason to get paid special for anything that carries the word *special* with it.

I got stuff—you saw it. I got things you need." Rosie smiled. A man walked up and carefully delivered his shirt and rifle to him.

"Yeah, double pay." The sheriff hadn't waited long to answer. "Just make sure you earn it."

Rosie smiled and walked away.

Later that afternoon he went to the small tent that was the first aid station. He found Washington Jones there, blissed out on painkillers and wrapped with white bandages around his chest—pure, clean cloth in dramatic contrast to his black skin.

"Bro," Rosie greeted him. "Guess I got carried away."

Jones looked up at him with a glaze across his eyes. "You a mean bastard. But you got *bad* moves. 'Sides, this means I get my pay, and I ain't got to do nothing but pop them happy pills. I shoulda learned that gook fighting stuff when I was in 'Nam, man. That was evil shit."

Rosie wondered if the man would be so accommodating if he wasn't strung out on medication. Maybe. In his limited vision, the fact that chemicals were being freely given to him because of the fight meant that Rosie was responsible for him getting to a source for his junk. Rosie studied Jones, and as he did, he wondered, as he often would, if he would have been in the other man's place if . . . So many *ifs*. If there hadn't been the Black Berets in 'Nam, if Beeker hadn't saved his life during the battle for Khe Sahn. If, if, if . . .

But a man can't deal with *ifs*. A man has to deal with what goes on in his world. His world still needed more information. Rosie took out a joint and lit it, then offered it to Jones. The other man inhaled, even though the effort obviously hurt. He coughed quickly, as though he was a kid taking his first toke.

"So who else is here, bro?" Rosie asked. He'd done some quick surveying himself, but there was only a little time and he'd only gotten a few things out of the other men.

"My bloods, they'll be pissed at you," Jones said, not realizing that the other black vets had automatically switched their allegiance to Rosie once he'd won their fight. "What else you want to know?"

"Well, I see they got some guys from LA . . ."

"Drifters, man, you know the kind, move along with the harvest, with them migrants, the ones that steal the money the pickers get after they work the crops, the ones that fuck the women, beat up on the men.

"That's all the spics is, leeches that were around. Everyone's just men that was around. Got some rednecks, got some dudes was out of money 'cause of the casinos. Just got the bad ones." Jones attempted another drag on the marijuana. This time it stayed down a little easier. "Just got a lot of bad dudes that know how to use guns and fists and want some cash money." Jones handed the joint to Rosie and leaned back on his pillows. "You better watch out for the blood brothers, man. They going to get you for what you did to me."

Rosie looked down at him and shook his head sadly. He was glad it'd worked this way, just a fight with their fists. He would have hated to kill Washington Jones. It would have been as meaningful as killing a dumb animal.

Rosie walked back through the camp to the barracks. He took his cot and laid down. Fifty bad men. Armed. Ready, even anxious to fight. For what?

# 12

Marty was being theatrical in his own way. He and Harry were near the bottom of Shaft 563 of the Nevari Piute Mine. The only light in the tunnel came from the battery-powered lamps attached to their hard hats. Wherever their heads faced, there was a ray of light. Everything else was pitch-black.

Marty just couldn't stop talking, but that wasn't anything new. "Harry," he whispered, "this is great. I mean, look at us, doing just what Beeker said to do. Go get a job in the mines, find out what's going on. We're fabulous, Harry. Look at us, investigating just the way Beak said and doing it in record time."

There was a conveyer belt moving beside them, taking out the big chunks of ore that men farther up were putting on it. They were only mechanics, only responsible for the working of the belt.

"What do you think it is, Harry? Huh? I bet it's commies."

Harry looked at his partner. The light from his hat reflected off Appelbaum's ever-present glasses. "Dust bothering you?" Harry asked.

Marty stiffened. "Harry, come on, don't bring that shit up."

Marty was always in danger of asthma. He also had a fear of enclosed spaces. Harry had wondered on more than one occasion if that's why the little guy liked to blow up buildings so much, to be able to take down the walls that might make him scared. "If I don't think about it," Marty whined, "then I'll be okay. But if you keep bringing it up . . ." He perked up again quickly, "But really, Harry, what do you think is going on?"

Harry looked around them. The mine was insufferably hot. The big, hairy Greek always sweat a lot, but in this stifling, torrid space he might as well be swimming. It wasn't just his armpits soaking his shirt—the whole damn thing was drenched.

"I think," Harry said very seriously, "that what's going on here is . . ."

"Yeah, yeah?" Appelbaum encouraged him to go on.

"Coal mining."

"Ah, Harry." Appelbaum was hurt more than angry. He hated it when his friend wouldn't play along with his sense of adventure. It made life too boring. He turned back to the conveyer belt and absent-mindedly picked through some of the pieces of ore.

It only took a couple of minutes for Marty to get his wind back though. "Look, Harry, didn't we luck out with the redskins? Huh, man, I bet no one else could have gotten in good with those savages the way you and me did."

Harry looked at Marty with the same deadened expression as always. He knew it was a good thing he didn't display emotions, especially around Marty, where it would have been disastrous. Harry didn't know what Marty would think if the little man knew how often he was astonished by Appelbaum's ignorance. "Savages?"

Marty could talk about "niggers" in front of Rosie, and then turn around and expect no one to notice that he'd used a word like "Injun" to describe Beeker or Tsali.

"I like Big Arrow. Like him a lot," Harry said.

"Yeah, you always like them. The ones that are different. I suppose that's something in your favor." Marty continued to play with the ore.

It was, obviously, in Marty's favor that Harry was interested in people no matter how much others might dislike them. But it wasn't going to do any good to point that out to the runt. Harry continued to stand silent.

He did like Big Arrow. He and the Indian man could sit for hours in a bar and just have a good time staring at the wall with one another. Big Arrow had the same capacity for ignoring bothersome intrusions, like Marty's constant yapping. It had only taken him a short while to pick up Harry's gift of appearing to listen to Appelbaum without allowing a single word to slip into his mind.

A sharp siren blew. There were two short blasts. Quitting time. "Oh man, time to get something to eat, something to drink, and something to screw. Harry, I am *ready*." Appelbaum was always ready to claim he was ready to screw. Of course, he had almost never been seen even walking into a bedroom with a woman, but that was one of the many details of Appelbaum's life Harry was willing to overlook.

The two men waited for a short while, until there was a clearing in the clumps of coal on the conveyer belt, then they jumped on. It was illegal but common for the miners to catch a ride. So long as the federal inspectors didn't see you, no one cared. And the federal inspectors got to a mine like this one about once every five years.

Still, for the sake of appearances, the two Black Berets did the same as other men, and jumped off when they got close enough to the big freight elevator. Big Arrow and two of his sons were already in the big wooden cage, waiting for more men to compose a full load.

Harry and Marty got on and stood beside their new friend. Harry and Big Arrow were content to nod. Marty couldn't be so easily satisfied. "Hey, Big A, how they hanging?" Marty beamed while he said that. As he so often did, the older Indian man just grunted a noncommittal response.

Marty turned to Big Arrow's sons. "Sam, Jack, how you doing?" They were both in their early twenties, seemingly happy to have anglicized names. No one had ever mentioned their origin. Harry suspected some missionary interference with the old ways, but he wasn't about to make an issue of it; Harry hardly ever made an issue of things.

The two sons began to talk to Marty. They were a natural trio. They were all for talking about skirts and wages, how much beer they'd drink that night, how much snatch they'd get. For them, it wasn't so bad; they were the age for that kind of talk. Harry studied them for a minute and wondered if he wasn't giving them too much when he thought they were twenty or so.

They had rough skin, but growing up in the stark wasteland and working in a mine would do that to you pretty quickly. They had young bodies, though, and younger minds, minds that fit right with Marty's. They really might only be in their late teens.

Harry looked at Big Arrow again. That might explain it. If a man had to live with two hotheaded young men like this all day and night, working and sharing a cabin with them, no woman around to take care of things, then he'd have learned how to shut them off. That's why Big Arrow could deal with Marty well enough.

"The twins?" Harry asked Big Arrow.

The Indian wasn't given to much emotion, at least nothing that would show. But a quick wave of exhaustion came over his face. "Yes," he replied.

Yep, Harry knew it then. Two of them, the same age, going

through the same cycles and stages, probably constantly fighting with one another, or else constantly fighting every other kid on the block. It would be enough to turn a sane man into a saint. That was it.

"Mother?" Harry had never asked about Big Arrow's wife before.

The Indian didn't seem to mind. "Left when they were four."

Harry studied the pair of them. He could see that the resemblance really was stronger than it would be for two regular brothers.

They were chatting away fast and furious with Marty, explaining their future plans. "Going to be going to apprentice school next month. Man, we're going to get us a job!" Jack started.

"A real job! We're going to be blasters." Whenever one of the brothers started talking, the other one inevitably ended up finishing.

"Bombs!" Marty said enthusiastically. "Well," his voice changed slightly, and his thin chest blew out a bit. "If you guys are lucky, you might end up working with me."

"You?" Jack asked.

"What's it got to do with you?" Sam continued.

"I just happen to be the maestro of demolition," Marty crowed.

"Then what you doing just working mechanics?" Sam said, obviously not believing what Marty was telling him.

"Yeah, why aren't you doing some blasting?" Jack wasn't buying it either.

"It's just that they got to check out my licenses, my credentials. Once they do, man, move your ass, you're going to see some *perfect* demolitions."

Harry knew it was a bad situation. Here was Marty, so close to a legal and honest way to be blowing things up it must hurt him not to be able to do it right away. Then, add to that an audience of two who were capable of actually respecting that skill of his, and more, just a touch of skepticism on their part . . . the bragging was going to start.

"Let me tell you what I did in Kentucky, when they really had to have some *amazing* demolition work on a coal mine. You know, I didn't really care about the danger. Hell, any job's got its danger. Of course, no one else would do it."

"Why?"

"How come?" The questions came so fast that Harry wasn't sure which one was Jack's and which was Sam's.

"You'll see, just listen. Anyway, if this stuff wasn't placed just right, there was some possibility—well, actually, it was a sure thing—that this children's hospital would have been swallowed into the ground. An inch to the right, the kids would go. Couldn't be moved—paralyzed, on life-support systems. But if the thing wasn't blasted, then, of course, the fire would have gotten to them eventually."

"You're shitting me!"

"Hey, how did you do that?" Again, the twins acted in pure harmony.

"You have your truck here?" Harry asked Big Arrow.

The Indian nodded.

"How about letting them go on together. You and me'll go and get a beer?"

"Wonderful." Relief crawled over Big Arrow's forehead. "Fuckin' wonderful."

It was the same bar they'd met in. The big neon sign out front called it Frankie's Restaurant, but Harry'd never seen anyone eat anything more than a microwaved hot dog in the place. It was a cavernous room, one of the big workingmen's bars you could find on the outskirts of any mining or industrial town. A place where men came and drank their beer, told their stories, and found a moment of peace and quiet between the demands of work on one side and home, wife, and children on the other.

Harry and Big Arrow got a pitcher of Miller and sat at one of the small tables with two glasses. Alone—no Marty, no Sam, no Jack. Peace.

It didn't make any difference if Waylon Jennings was playing at earsplitting decibel levels; it didn't bother them that there might be a friendly fistfight every now and then, or that there was almost always some kind of sporting event on the projected TV screen with a commentary going just high enough to compete with Waylon's sighs of unrequited love.

This was how men relaxed.

Harry wasn't even going to get upset that Ron was there, in a cluster of other guys in a corner of the room, listening to someone speaking. The speaker was standing on a chair—he had a lot of men around him and evidently decided he needed the height.

Harry wondered what was going on. Big Arrow was nodding out in his own way—not falling asleep but savoring his beer and that special kind of solitude a man gets in a barroom.

Harry stood, catching Big Arrow's eye, and said, "Be back."

The Indian grunted in response.

The Greek took a full glass of Miller over to the corner. He didn't notice anything special about any of the men—they were just the usual type of regulars for Frankie's. Ron saw him and moved to the farther edge of the group. He probably hadn't gotten over the humiliation of having lost that fight to a runt like Marty; he was embarrassed to be seen by a witness.

The man on the makeshift podium was in his early fifties, older than the rest of them. He was wearing a white shirt and a cowboy tie underneath a polyester suit, the cheap kind where the stitching showed too clearly.

"I tell you, men, this is just a plot. A plot to take away the jobs and the livelihoods of good American men. I tell you, the only way that we can fight this conspiracy is with fire. Fire meets fire, and the devil gets burnt!"

The crowd murmured appreciatively. Harry had seen lots of graffiti and other indications that the people of Mesa County were getting scared of the court case they'd lost. He figured this guy was just feeding off that fear. He wondered how he intended to make it work for himself.

"Do you think that the savages, the ones that won this case, are going to be satisfied with just land? You know they won't. They are the un-Christian ones. You know that. You've seen that heathen Small Eagle get on television and say that all of *us* were the savages. He dared say that! We know that there are some decent souls on that Coyote Clan reservation. They were saved by the missionaries. Unable to help themselves and the weak genes that led them to drunkenness and lewdness, they'd given their lives to Christ.

"But Small Eagle and his band of Native American Crusaders"—the speaker's voice dripped with hatred—"have given up their one chance to be civilized. They've turned on Jesus Christ and given their hearts back to their idols."

The appreciative sounds were louder now. Harry thought that a revival meeting in a bar was sort of strange, but he'd certainly seen much stranger things in his life.

"You watch, you hear me, you pay attention to what I say. They're without Jesus now. Without Jesus, they have no morals. Without God, they have no restraints. They think they won your land. Now they'll want your women. After that, your country."

Harry sipped his beer and tried to imagine Jack, Sam, and Big Arrow wanting to do much with anything more than their cabin and a few extra acres of land that might be good enough to bring in some vegetables, maybe some grassland that would sustain a goat or two, maybe some sheep.

"They're going to be on the move!" the quasi-evangelist went on. "And when they start, you had better be ready."

A couple of the men actually applauded that. Harry listened carefully and heard some of the words they were using: *Guns. Rifles. Protection.*

He went back to Big Arrow and took a chair again. He looked over at the group that had broken into smaller units, two or three men talking excitedly with each other. "Big Arrow, you in the Native American Crusade?"

The older man laughed as loud as Harry had ever heard him. "Hell no. I don't want to live on some piece of dust with a mouthful of tough goat meat and no clothes on. That's all those guys do."

"But you're full-blooded Coyote Clan, right?"

"Damn right," Big Arrow said proudly.

"You born on the reservation?"

"I was. Got married there too. Still registered for all my rights when the court case comes through."

"What's this Crusade got to do with things?"

"Bunch of old ladies and some good kids. That's all. The court case—you know all about that—that's being handled by the tribal council. My friend White Wind, he's on that. He's the one that helped get it through."

Big Arrow took more beer. "I think it'll make a lot of difference to work in a mine that the tribe owns. We're going to own that thing, too, once White Wind gets it all cleared up."

"But the Native American Crusade, they're on TV—"

"They just want some playtime. White Wind's son, he's the head of it, sure. But he's got nothing to do with the tribal council. That's elected by the whole Coyote Clan."

"Why's that guy so hot and bothered by the Crusade, then?" Harry nodded to the men in the corner.

Big Arrow frowned. "People don't like different things, that's all. Buncha kids and women go up on the sacred mesa and you'd think they were pulling a revolution. Hell, the real revolution is the one happening in the courts. They're just full of sour grapes. Forget 'em."

Harry didn't think that was the wisest idea he'd heard. In a bit, the two of them went next door to a hamburger joint and got something to eat. It was only a Tuesday, but Harry insisted he wanted to go back to Frankie's. Big Arrow wasn't accustomed to staying out this late, but if his friend wanted to, he'd keep him company. Man shouldn't drink alone.

When they walked into Frankie's this time, Marty and the twins were there. There was a trio of pitchers on their table. As usual, Marty wasn't showing any effects from alcohol. Maybe he had a looser tongue, but it would be hard to know, Marty's tongue already being so loose.

Sam and Jack, though, were ready to slide under the table. Big Arrow looked at them and the boozed-up smirks on their faces and shook his head. "Only eight o'clock—look at 'em."

"Pa, this man is a genius. Do you know what he did to the Grand Canyon?" Jack was the one speaking.

"No, and I don't think I care to find out. Come on, get your asses up off the chairs and let's go home." He grabbed each of his sons by the collar of his shirt and lifted. The boys weren't in any shape to resist, that was obvious.

They smiled at Marty, and one of them said, "I want to hear more about that mine in Africa, the diamonds. Jesus, man, that's—"

Harry cut Sam short. "Diamonds in Africa?"

"Well . . . um . . ." Marty looked uncomfortable all of a sudden.

"Night." Big Arrow saved him by dragging his sons out the door.

Harry looked at his watch. He and Big Arrow had only been gone a short while, less than an hour. There was already a whole line of shot glasses on the table as well as the three pitchers of beer. He lifted one up and smelled.

"Bourbon?"

"Only way for a man to drink a good beer is with a shot!" Marty declared. But his statement was undercut by a loud belch.

"Marty, they were kids! What are you doing getting kids drunk like that?"

"Hey, they're man enough to work in the mines, they're man enough to drink like men." Marty burped once more.

"Well, you better start drinking like the undercover guy you're supposed to be." Harry picked up the one pitcher that still had some beer left and poured himself a glass. "I want to check some stuff out tonight."

"What, Harry? What is it?"

"We had a preacher in here tonight, talking about the need to have the white men armed."

"Against the commies? That makes sense."

Harry closed his eyes and remembered a short Greek prayer his mother used to say when she really needed a strong dose of patience. "Marty, anyone who arms himself in this place at this time just might end up using those arms against us or Beeker. Remember Beeker? Billy Leaps? Our leader? The guy we promised we'd help out when he came to work for his Indian friend against the bad white guys in Mesa County?"

"Oh yeah," Marty said sheepishly. "Sure, so? What's up?"

"I don't think the preacher's the only one that's going to work this crowd tonight. I think we're going to have more visitors.

All kinds. I want to know what they're saying and how they're saying it."

"Got it," Marty said. He stood up and reached over for one of the empty pitchers.

"Stay away from that Ron guy. If you left him any balls, he might want to pay you back for what you did to his pal."

"Him?" Marty said sarcastically. "I don't have to watch out for him or any other white guy. We're on Beak's side this trip out, like you said. White men are scum this trip out."

Harry didn't bother to point out that the two of them were white. It was better to let Marty find his own strange kind of logic in their identities for right now.

The night did prove strange and interesting. There were, as Harry had suspected, many different kinds of men who came in. They were classic provocateurs.

There had been the union men, supposedly. They spread rumors designed to make the men angry: The Coyote Clan would wipe out the seniority system Nevari had given them. That they were going to take all the supervisory jobs and expect white men to make up for a century of neglect by being the lowest on the totem pole.

There was a group of men who came in and had stories to tell. Harry checked on most of them and discovered that his suspicions were right. None of them worked at the Nevari mines, and very few of them were regulars. But they had tales to tell that people were ready to hear. About white women being raped. These were always embellished with details about the Coyote Clan men who did the raping, telling the women that they could expect more of the same now that the region was going to be turned over to them.

Then there were a couple of men who came in and complained that members of the Coyote Clan were jumping the gun and beginning to show up on white men's property, sizing it up and telling the rightful owners that their hard-earned homes were going to be turned into hogans.

The rumor-spreading was skillful. There was always a bit of truth to what was being said, enough that a man at all inclined to believe the stories could hold on to. There was always the possibility that even a sane man who heard enough of them from enough different sources would start to feel the paranoia.

Harry and Marty kept on going at the beer. They listened and they moved through the various groups. Some of them were friendly to one or the other. The ones who were the most hysterical, the ones who not only believed what they were told but exaggerated it when they turned around to tell their neighbors, tended to recognize a kindred soul in Marty.

Others, those who didn't want to believe the stories but wondered what was going on, took refuge with Harry's calm presence. Not that it was going to be enough to soothe them for long. There was a panic growing in the group. A real sense of doom.

"But the government said they'd reach an accommodation," one man had complained. "You know that. So Washington will have to pay out some money. They give it to everyone else. Why not the Coyote Clan?"

"So they can swill it down in cheap drink?" another guy complained.

"Who cares what the fuck they do with it. It'll be their money. Come on, we've all heard the secretary of the interior. He said it would work out."

"Yeah, but did you hear that Native American Crusade guy when he brought the national network in? He wants it all. Bastards are going to take our land, everything we have."

"We should have sent Cecelia Range to Washington, not just to the state capital in Carson City," one man said. Harry looked over—it was Ron. "She knows how to put the redskins in their place. Back on the reservation. It's bad enough the mines gotta hire more of them for the goddamn quotas."

"Those are our union's quotas," one man tried to point out.

"So, you're surprised the union's in the hands of the Coyote Clan too? Hell no, you shouldn't be. Those union guys know where the butter's going to be if the Coyote Clan takes it all away from us."

"We're going to end up working for the Indians like we were coolies or something. They're going to take away all our benefits."

"They're going to outlaw churches—I heard it on the radio. They're going to stop us from praising Jesus."

"They're going to . . ."

It went on that way all night. The men at Frankie's were building themselves up to a fever pitch.

# 13

Beeker stared out over the edge of the mesa. It was nearly ten o'clock. There were stars appearing in greater numbers in the sky. There was little to block them here. As on his farm in Louisiana, there was clean air, clean living available. Down below, off to the left somewhere, were mines and smelting plants. The beginning of the industrialization of even this wilderness.

Beeker had seen the big coal-burning power plants they'd constructed in the Southwest. He thought the amount of soot they'd thrown into the air was unimaginable.

He wondered quickly if the Coyote Clan couldn't take their land claims and turn this all back to a wilderness. A true wilderness. Just some men and their families, some animals . . . No, he knew they wouldn't do it. They wanted jobs, "education," and "advancement."

Tsali came up and stood beside his father, scanning the same horizon, searching out the same stars. Here, on this mesa, a long time ago, some warriors of the Coyote Clan had fought off the United States Army. They'd planted the seed for a victory they couldn't even dream of. Now, it might be up to Tsali and Beeker and a handful of people to hold out again, to fight again, to throw back another enemy. Beeker wondered what would come of the seed he might plant for the future.

Here, on the mesa, he might be doing something that would affect people a century later.

Why think that way? he reprimanded himself. Why do that?

It was better to continue to walk the edge of the mesa and find the weak link in the defense perimeter. He should be looking for the best place to put himself and the others for any attack that might come.

They had a handful of hunting rifles, and they'd gotten all the ammunition they could on such short notice by buying out a couple of the local stores. He had to get some decent weapons up here. He had to find the means to protect these people, and he had to trust the rest of the team to find out who the hell they were protecting the Coyote Clan from.

Sheriff Passak looked over his special squad. He was obviously pleased. "Now, you have to understand that we need you for this assignment because we can't take the chance of one of my own men being caught up in the fun and games you're going on. That's why you're useful to me. That's why you're all getting your bonuses.

"You understand what you're to do?"

Rosie was one of the six men who nodded. One of the others had been introduced to him as Rico Ambrosino. He was Italian, from the Bronx, New York. Rico had some trouble with the gaming tables at Vegas. But he'd found a friend who knew a friend who understood that Sheriff Passak could use some experienced help.

But Rico was probably surprised to find out just what kind of help he was supposed to be. The big man's hairy chest and puffed-up arms were open to inspection. He was wearing an incredible costume of Adidas sneakers, a swimmer's racing suit, and a loincloth purchased at the kind of Indian curio shoppe that had imported all its goods from Taiwan. Around his big bicep were straps of rawhide, maybe the only authentic thing on his body. His face was ludicrously painted up in a Hollywood version of what an Indian was supposed to look like. There were streaks of red, white, and green paint on his cheeks and his forehead. His curly hair hadn't been straightened.

No one would ever mistake this guy for a real Indian. But, of course, the only people who were going to be alive to do that were a couple of deputies, and it had been all arranged for them to only "observe" the renegades from a distance.

"You got the target? You know what to do?" Sheriff Passak asked.

They all nodded, but Rosie doubted that any of them knew just as much as he did who the targets were. At least, he doubted they knew who the targets were.

The sheriff went through the diversion again. As he explained the location of the tiny village they were going to attack, Rosie studied the others some more. The fact their costumes were ridiculous didn't change the reality that they were a powerful group of men. He wondered just what it was that bound them together, made them the choice for this mission.

There was Rico. There were two Mexicans named Garcia and Mantez. And a roustabout redneck named Biker—the only name he'd give or answer to—and his pal Speed.

Rosie realized they were all supposed to be like Washington Jones. They were all a little insane—the ones who had forgotten the limits of society or else chose to ignore them. They were accepting an assignment to exterminate a small community of innocent people without any compunction. It was one thing to accept the idea that you had to do that when you were in an army. When you were in a place like 'Nam and you discovered that the little kids were shooting at you with their mama-sans, you shot back. But you should remember to cry for the babies when you did it. Even Rosie had cried for them.

Those kids shouldn't have been caught in a thing like a war. They should have grown up and cultivated rice and made babies from lots and lots of good loving. That's what life should have meant for those people. But they got caught, and Rosie still wasn't sure what they had been caught in.

These were the kind of guys who would have gone after those kids in 'Nam with a smile on their faces and not a single tear afterward.

They were certainly willing to do it tonight. Fake Indians, they were going after real people. They thought.

When the sheriff had finished speaking, the men lined up without any real formation and walked to the waiting pickup truck that was to drive them to Five Corners, the town they were supposed to massacre. They all had their Mini-14s with them. Extra magazines were tucked in the belts they were using to hold up their "loincloths."

Rosie leaned back against the metal side of the bed of the truck and looked the others over. There were two sheriff's deputies in the cab. The men were silent as they were driven over the rutted back roads of the county. They were absolutely unaffected by what they were about to do.

"Hey, any of you guys know anything about this scalping thing? I mean, just how do you do it?" Rico yelled over the truck's noise.

"You just take a knife and cut off the top of their head," Biker said.

"No, no." Rosie smiled. He knew about this. "You got to do it just right for it to be real, man, just right. You see, you got to take your knife, real sharp now, and you got to slice around the top of their heads, deep, real deep. Then you lift up. Pull the hair. Be careful—you always seem to get an artery, and they bleed all over the place. But you pull up on their hair and then you take the point of the knife and you sort of dig in underneath what's left there and you dig some more and then it sort of just *peels* off."

He leaned back and smiled after delivering that little lecture. He got great satisfaction from watching the faces of the men, especially Spike, whose pale complexion had gotten noticeably paler.

They were quiet after that and didn't bother him. That was good. Rosie didn't want to talk to any of these men anymore. What he'd heard was enough. He was worried that if they opened their yaps, one of them might actually say something close to human, and if he did, well, then it would be harder on Rosie later on.

The truck came to a slow stop. They climbed out of the back and looked ahead. There, not far away, were the houses of Five Corners. There were actually only that same number: five. The place barely made the grade as a village. Rosie was surprised it even could claim to have a name of its own.

"Go to it," smiled an encouraging deputy as he stepped out of the cab. "It's all yours, Kimosabes!"

"Hey, man, you got class." Rico smiled at the deputy and slapped his shoulder. "Let's move it!" he said to the others.

They moved forward, leaving the two deputies behind. As soon as they'd gone far enough to be out of earshot of the deputies, Rosie stopped them all. "Hell, I forgot my scalping knife. I got so hot and bothered telling you all about it."

"We don't have time," complained Biker. "Forget it."

"I told that sheriff that I do things right, or I don't do them at all." Rosie was insistent.

"Go ahead, then. We'll wait here. Just hurry." Rico had

decided he was in command of the group. No one felt like challenging him.

Rosie stood and ran back toward the truck. The deputies were smoking cigarettes outside it, leaning against the back of the bed. Rosie smiled when he saw them. *Easy.*

He moved quickly again. He wore moccasins that made little sound on the rock, but the deputies were talking, and that would have covered his noise anyway. "I gotta take a leak," one of them said. He moved a few yards away and turned his back on his compatriot.

Rosie moved like lightning. His knife was in his hands—he'd lied to the others. He jumped on the nearer of the guards, and he jammed a forearm up against his jaw, making any movement or speech impossible. He had the man's head lifted straight up and back. It left his Adam's apple wide open. Before he could think to do more than try to pry off the offending arm, his hands grabbing frantically at the black skin of Rosie's grip, Rosie's other hand came up and carved a quick, deep line from ear to ear.

Rosie let the man collapse onto the ground. If he was, possibly, alive enough to still speak, his voice was cut off by the flood of blood gushing in pumping geysers from his wound.

Rosie covered the short distance to the other man in the same quick movements. "Hey, I tell you, I must have loaded my bladder with that cheap beer at Frankie's," the deputy said. He didn't realize he was speaking to only Roosevelt Boone.

Rosie was behind him just as he'd finished unzipping his fly and reached in to bring out his pecker. Rosie couldn't help himself; he had to laugh. But he wasn't as worried about noise now. He took the blunt end of his knife and hit the deputy on the back of his skull, hard enough to knock him out.

The deputy came to not long after. He was on his back, a

black man straddling his chest. The deputy felt that surge of adrenaline go through his body that a man got when danger insisted that he react beyond his capacity. He was fully conscious as soon as he opened his eyes. But then he was flooded with stimuli. There was something wet running down his upper chest. But the deputy was lucky. He passed out before he could know that the big black man named Roosevelt Boone had carved a nice arc along the edge of his throat.

Rosie stood up. It was time to go back to the other men. He jogged toward the place he had left them. He got to the point where he was sure they should have been, but couldn't find them. They'd started!

Damn. He checked the rifle in his hand one more time. He moved cautiously toward the lighted windows of Five Corners. He could make out two silhouettes. He didn't know which men they were, but their white skin picked up the light from the window. Their legs were bare. Rosie had to assume these were two of the attackers. No townspeople should be wandering around without pants on at this time of night.

Rosie was too far away to take the chance the men weren't going to start their gruesome assignment before he could get to them with his hands and eliminate them without the noise of his gun. He decided he'd just have to do it differently. He was more willing to take this chance than to sacrifice some innocent kids' lives.

He put the stock of the Mini-14 to his shoulder. It had a dim-light scope just for this occasion. He sighted and pulled off two rounds quickly at the first of the men, the one right in front of the window. Then, before the other one could react, he shot off two more rounds. The first target had simply slumped to the ground after he'd bounced onto the wall. Rosie knew he must have hit him in the chest. The second one, though, Rosie shot a little high. Just the reflecting light from the house made it clear enough that his two bullets had shattered the man's skull.

The four shots were more than enough of an alert for everyone involved. Rosie dropped to the ground. He hoped to hell that there were some men in that village who knew how to handle a gun, who understood that rifle fire this close meant the kind of trouble that made you put your kids and your wife in safe places.

Rosie began to crawl crab style on the dirt, moving toward the village. He saw two more of the men running away from the houses. They were identifiable in the moonlight once they got away from the immediate illumination from the houses.

There was another man, but this one clearly in full clothing, not one of the attackers, running around to chase after them. The man had some kind of rifle; he stood his ground, aimed, and got off two shots. Both men fell forward.

Whoever that guy was, Rosie was happy that kind of marksman was on his side. He moved toward the spot where the two bodies had fled.

Well, he decided once he got there, maybe the guy wasn't that good after all. It was Biker and his pal Spike. They'd both been hit, but their wounds would only be superficial. Biker was already crawling back toward the village, probably wanting to take revenge for the inconvenience of the bullet wound in his leg. Spike had taken some lead in his shoulder. Rosie could see he was ready to follow his friend. Spike was the kind who would be happy to take a little pain if he could get even for it.

If the guys had gotten away, it might have been all right. Maybe they would have just taken this as an omen of the problems that were only starting. But now, with their egos and their bodies in pain, they were going to be hard-assed.

Rosie had no choice. He was going to have to be hard-assed

too. He moved to Spike first. All the other guy's attention was taken up by the brave house owner. He was watching as Biker made his way back. Rosie was able to move up on Spike quickly and slip his ready, bloodied knife into Spike's lung and pull it in a tearing motion across the man's chest. Spike's jaw opened, but the knife had made sure there wasn't any air left to allow any sound to warn Biker.

Then Rosie took his rifle, and aimed it carefully, up on one knee. He perched his Mini-14 on the other and squeezed off a single shot. Biker rose up, arcing his back and screaming in a way Rosie had heard in 'Nam—the kind of scream that meant it was all over. The man had bought his last ticket.

But that meant there was still one left. Who was it, and where was he?

The villager had no way of knowing who was doing the shooting and at whom. He was taking what cover he could from one of the scrawny trees in his backyard. He was staring out into the blackness and wondering what the hell was going to come at him next. Biker's scream had freaked him, made him too nervous. There was no way he was going to be able to believe that Rosie was on his side if the black man tried to get his attention.

Then Rosie saw Rico. He was moving up the side of the house. He'd spotted the villager and was getting ready to take his own shot. He would be as confused by all that had gone on as the other man. All he'd know was this was one of them, one of the enemy they'd been sent to get.

Rosie watched the whole thing as it started to roll out. He could see the inevitable. Rico was going to kill the man. Rosie had nothing but respect for the dude; he'd only been protecting his property, probably his children and his wife. He'd done it pretty well, hurting two vicious men who would have gladly killed him.

Rosie wasn't going to let it happen. The sight lines were lousy, but they were all he had to work with. He made his quick calculations and decided to take his chances. Just as Rico was taking his final aim, Rosie stood up, his rifle at his shoulder, and pumped out five rounds of the Mini-14 bullets. Rico yelled in mortal agony. The rounds all hit his left side. He dropped his rifle and staggered into the bright light of the closest window. His left shoulder had been all but cut off by the tumbling .223s.

Rosie was so intent on the melodrama of Rico's hit and the collapse the Italian man made onto the ground that he forgot the villager for a split second too long. The man had no idea what or who Rosie was shooting at. It certainly must have seemed like the black man with only a loincloth on was aiming at him. He took his hunting rifle, and before Rosie could regain himself, there was a shot.

Burning, searing pain shot through Rosie's side. He'd been hit!

# 14

There was a knock on the door. At first Harry thought it must be Marty. Maybe the guy'd forgotten his key to the room they'd rented. But as soon as he was awake enough to think, he realized that Marty was snoring away on his own bed just a couple of feet away.

Harry threw his legs off the side of his own mattress and stumbled toward the door. "Who is it?"

"Big Arrow."

*What the hell was this guy doing here? At this time of night?*

Harry opened the door and let his friend in. He glanced over at the clock on the nightstand. It read fifteen after midnight. "What's up?" He trusted Big Arrow not to be making a meaningless social call.

"My sons. They've gone to the mesa."

Harry looked at his friend and tried to decipher his message. "So?"

"The mesa, where the Native American Crusade people are. There's trouble. There's going to be more. The young men are going to the mesa, hoping it's a good place to fight."

"Fight?" Harry went over to his clothes, spread out on one of the scrawny hotel chairs. "Fill me in, Big Arrow. Tell me what's going on. I don't understand."

"That's why I need you, Harry. I need you to go to town and find out just that. My boys, I don't want them in trouble. But I don't dare go to Frankie's or anyplace else. It's not safe for a Coyote Clan member, or any Indian. You got to go and see what's happening."

"Get up." Harry shoved at Marty's still-snoring body. The little man sat up quickly, the covers falling off his chest. Harry looked down at him and wondered, as he often did, how such skin and bones could be so strong when it had to be. Sometimes it looked like the pale white skin on Appelbaum's chest was curving inward, not out.

"What the fuck! Hey, Harry, what are you doing? Don't you know how dangerous it is to wake up a SEAL that way."

"Yeah, yeah, I was one, too, remember?" That's where they'd met, in training for the Navy's elite fighting unit. One of the myths about SEALs was the danger in waking them. It was rumored that the only safe way was to tickle their feet and run like hell.

"Come on, Marty, get dressed. We got more business at Frankie's. Maybe all the way in town."

"Now? Hell, Harry, we got to go to work at seven."

"I think we got to go to work right now. Big Arrow, you think your house is safe?"

"I don't know. I just don't know. If they find out that my sons went to the mesa—"

"You stay here till we get back," Harry said. "I don't care how late that is; you stay right here. If a man like you thinks it's dangerous to walk the streets of Mesa City or go to Frankie's, I believe him."

Marty was pulling up his jeans. "Harry, what we got for weapons? What we going to use tonight?"

"Bring out the M16s."

Big Arrow's eyes widened as Marty pulled out a chest and opened it. He unwrapped two long parcels. Inside were two government-issue rifles. Marty methodically pulled out clips of ammunition for them. "Harry, are you sure—"

"Go ahead, take it too. I guess you're going to have to have it nearby. Just don't expect me to carry the fucker."

If Big Arrow had been surprised at the rifles, he was even more shocked to see the next package. It was even more carefully wrapped in the kind of padded covers movers used. Inside he recognized an M60, a lethal automatic that seemed almost as large as Marty. "Oh, baby." The little blond man ran a hand up and down the stock of the weapon.

"Watch out you don't get a hard-on," Harry said. He never quite understood little Marty's love affair with M60s. He knew the man loved them. "Get them to the rental car. We're going. Fast."

They finished dressing and loaded up the car, carefully concealing the M60 and one of the M16s in the trunk. Harry put the other rifle on the floor of the back seat and camouflaged it with one of the packing blankets.

They closed the car doors and raced toward Frankie's. Harry knew something was wrong as soon as they arrived. There were hardly any cars in the parking lot. It was too early for the bar to be empty.

They locked the car and walked inside. The music was playing, and there was a cable program on, some kind of European football to take up the late-night screen and let the cable network claim it had twenty-four-hour programming. But there weren't many of the regulars.

"Be cool, calm down," Harry said to Marty. He didn't want the excitable little man to blow it for them. They went to the bar. Marty tried, Harry knew the man was trying, but it wasn't working that well. He was squirming on his stool, just so anxious and raring to go that he couldn't hide it much longer.

As soon as the bartender came back with the two beers Harry had ordered, the Greek threw him the question, "Where's everyone?"

"You work at the mine, don't you?"

Harry could see the suspicion in the bartender's eye. "Yeah."

"Well, I suppose you should know. There's been more trouble. A lot more trouble. Some Indians went and shot up one of the white villages. Got a lot of people hurt. Some dead. Then there was another explosion—this one at the Mesa Piute operation. Word spread that everyone should go and find out what to do there."

"The Piute Mine?" That was where Marty and Harry had been working.

"You got it. Some men on the late shift are caught. They're afraid they're dead. Or dying. It's the Coyote Clan. They're going too far. Those radicals of theirs—that Native American Crusade—they're behind it. Word is that Senator Range is going to the mine right now. God knows, Cecelia will figure out how to handle this. Damn Indians."

Harry was glad Big Arrow was back in the hotel. He drank half the beer in his glass, then turned to Marty, who'd finished his. "Time to go. We got to check this out."

"Mr. Hatcher?"

Cowboy had his usual trouble recognizing his name through the telephone receiver. It was especially difficult when he'd been sound asleep, and the ringing telephone had woken him up. His name finally registered. "Yeah."

"Maria Vasquela. Mr. Hatcher, we have an emergency. We need you to fly the corporate jet to Nevada tonight."

"Tonight! For Christ's sake, it's after midnight."

"Mr. Hatcher." Vasquela's voice was exasperated. "I didn't think I'd have to remind you of the bonus pay that a Nevari pilot gets for overtime, and still more that he gets for night flights. I have the company car and driver on their way to pick me up. We'll come by and get you as soon as possible. Be waiting outside your apartment building, if you don't mind the inconvenience." She hung up the phone.

Cowboy was dressed in his usual costume when the stretch Cadillac limousine pulled up to the curb. The back door opened, Maria Vasquela's hand on the handle. He climbed in and pulled the door shut after himself.

"What's the deal?" he asked, exaggerating a yawn to express his displeasure over the time.

"The *deal*, Mr. Hatcher, is a major emergency at our mines in Mesa. There's been another bombing—this one involving potentially many deaths."

Cowboy stretched his eyebrows high and whistled softly. "Accident?"

"Hardly," she said. "It's the dirty Indians."

Cowboy stared at her. "That's a strange thing for you to complain about. I mean, by now most Mexicans—"

"I am not Mexican," she hissed. "I am Spanish. Don't insult me. You've gone too far with your remarks. I've chosen to overlook your crass behavior in my office, and the way you look at me. Don't deny it. I see the way you look at me whenever you can. I know that look on men's faces."

Maria Vasquela was showing a Latin temper for the first time since he'd met her. It was a decidedly unattractive one. But her one outburst told him lots. He sank back in the seat of the limo and realized that now he understood about Maria. The remark about being Spanish and not Mexican was a bit of racial make-believe a lot of Mexicans liked to fall into. They would claim pure bloodlines back to the conquistadores. They'd make believe that centuries of inbreeding with the natives of their country hadn't happened. They were above it all. The Indians were savages.

The Mexicans who bought that line were among the worst racists in the world. They didn't have any of the sugarcoating or at-least-they're-all-God's-children forgiveness that the worst of the Americans had. They just had naked hatred. It was blunt, direct, and ugly, even when it came from the mouth of a woman as beautiful as Maria Vasquela.

"But why would the Indians do it?" Cowboy decided to ignore the racial ugliness and to bring them back to the business at hand. "They won. It's going to be all theirs. Why would they blow it up?"

"None of it's going to be theirs," Maria said. A smile came over her at last. "Not a single inch of it. By the time things have happened, they won't even be willing to claim their old reservation. They can go off to the worst of the wasteland and eat cactus and get crazy on their peyote seeds. It's all they really deserve."

Cowboy didn't press the issue. He just sat silently as the big car sped through the Los Angeles traffic toward the airport where the plane was waiting for them.

Soon the Lear Jet was making its usual elegant ascent. Cowboy loved the bird. It was designed for the easiest kind of flying—no big loads, no overweight freight, none of the problems of armaments. It was just designed to carry a few bodies from point A to point B with the least turbulence, the greatest comfort, and more than adequate speed.

He got the plane up to a decent altitude. He leveled off

and put the Lear on automatic pilot. Then he reached over and switched on his little intercom.

". . . the timing's off, but the element of surprise is even greater this way." It was Adamson's voice.

"The group of fifty men is in place. I received the confirmation from Passak." Maria was being her usually efficient self.

"Good. Now it's up to Cecelia to add up the numbers. Those fifty men are only the spearhead. The others have to be mobilized."

"How are we going to neutralize the opposing forces? Surely—"

"*Surely*? Nothing is involved *surely* in this case. Well, perhaps the courts. Their ruling won't be overturned. But the courts have no power. When you have a situation like this one, then the people with that one essential ingredient—power—come into play.

"You've proven a loyal trouper, Vasquela. But you don't have the big picture. You see it all from Nevari's point of view. Well and good. You know damn well that we need the new mines . . ."

*New mines*: that perked up Cowboy's interest.

". . . but just think of the rest of them. All the multinationals stand to lose something in this deal if the Coyote Clan wins. There's hardly an oil-producing company in the United States that doesn't have some stake in that part of the country. But even the oil wealth is nothing compared to the water rights.

"If the Coyote Clan claims stand, they will own a share of the Colorado River. Not one single developer in Los Angeles or Phoenix or any city in between can stand a decrease in his city's water supply. Water's worth more than oil in this part of the country—"

"Though there are some things even more valuable than water, *anywhere*," Maria said, and laughed. "There are some things . . ."

Adamson joined in the laughter. "Yes, sometimes I'm amazed by that. To think that the Coyote Clan worshipped that old mesa for so long. They didn't even know what they were praying to. It's amazing. Amazing."

Cowboy clicked off the intercom and wondered what the hell the two of them were talking about.

Harry didn't have to wonder about the crowd gathered in front of the Piute Mine. The entrance to Shaft 563 was hidden behind a shield of canvas awning. Inside, the rumors agreed, was a blown-out mine shaft with at least twenty-five men in it.

All around them was the evidence of a disaster. There were emergency medical crews. The Red Cross had set up a field hospital. Harry got the creeps looking at it. It was just like the ones in Vietnam. The tented building and the uniformed doctors and nurses could have been in a medevac area back in Asia. But now the doctors and nurses stood around, a couple of them smoking cigarettes, carefully standing away from the oxygen tents. This was the place any rescued miners would be brought to.

Harry had seen his share of catastrophes, natural ones and man-made ones. He knew there was something missing from this scene.

There were the obligatory crowds of anxious people. Mainly, it was the men, the other miners, who always came and stood at a place like this, as they knew too well they could have been the ones trapped inside the earth. They thought their presence just might be enough to provide the energy for one of the guys to escape.

Then there were the wives and children. They were, as always, terrified that the miners would never return. With their deaths would come desolation. Harry looked at one little boy—he couldn't have been more than five—who was looking around at the milling crowd, wondering what the hell they had to do with his daddy. Why, the boy was crying, wasn't his daddy here?

A woman dressed in a cotton dress, which seemed to have come from a mail-order catalog, and hair that hadn't seen the inside of a styling parlor in many months pulled the boy up to her hip and held a hand on his brow, hoping it would give the little guy some comfort. She would have done more, but her other free hand was holding a crying infant wrapped in worn blankets. She was standing tall and keeping her composure, but there were tears making regular tracks down each of her cheeks.

Harry went over to her. "What's the word?"

She looked at the big Greek man. She shrugged. "My Bill's down there. Worked a double shift tonight. We needed the extra money." She looked down at her son. "We didn't need it this much. They say it's a bomb. They say it's the Coyote Clan did it. Don't make sense to me. Bill and me, we knew they were going to get what they wanted. Coyote Clan people never hurt us; we never hurt them. Bill said it'd be all right to work for the mine if they owned it. Can't see why they blew it up. Something is going on. Don't know what. Things are never what they seem—Bill always said that."

Harry reached down and picked up the little boy.

"Bill Junior," his mother said, a little pride showing through her tears. The towheaded boy stared at the stranger.

Harry felt like he was going to cry with the woman. Just holding this little boy, with his bloodshot blue eyes, made him sad. Kids shouldn't have to feel this, he thought. He was back to 'Nam, the way his memories took him back so often. He was holding a little Vietnamese boy who'd never see his family again. They were killed by a mortar round that went wide of the target and hit a perfectly peaceful village. Kids shouldn't be a part of war. Never.

The boy's hand reached out and touched Harry's unshaven cheek. The Greek's stubble was always incredibly thick, and it was raspy to the kid's touch. "You from television? I always see television when there's trouble. Is my daddy going to be on television?"

That was it! From the mouth of babes. "No, no. I'm just a miner like your daddy."

"My daddy's Big Bill Rakin. You know him? I'm going to be just like him when I grow up." The boy was easily distracted.

Harry wasn't. The television crews? Where were they? He put the child down and patted Mrs. Rakin on the arm. "Things will be okay."

She looked at him. He could tell she knew he was lying. He could also tell that she was grateful for it.

Harry went back to where Marty was standing. The Greek looked around and saw the meaning of the boy's question. Whenever there's a possibility of a human tragedy, there were always television crews to cover the event. None could be seen. The crowd was large. Harry grabbed Marty and began to move through the hundreds of people to see if the missing journalists could be spotted.

The whole area around the mine was brightly lit with harsh lights. The effect, in the middle of the dark night, was unworldly. There was so much illumination that the presence of something as visible as cameras shouldn't have gone unnoticed.

"Why aren't there TV cameras?" Harry asked out loud.

"I don't know," Marty said. He was pissed that the Greek had been ignoring him. "I never saw so many politicians and no press in my life." Marty made it sound as though he were the one being ignored by the journalists.

But he made Harry aware of the other inconsistency in the setting. There was a makeshift podium set up. Harry had thought that it was for public announcements. But he looked over and could see that there was a huge banner: CECELIA RANGE: HERE AT YOUR MOMENT OF NEED.

He could see some poster-sized pictures of the state senator. He recognized her photographs from leftover campaign leaflets that had been stuck up at Frankie's. Senator Range was obviously a popular politician in this area.

There was a scuffle going on at the side of the platform. Harry could make out a man he knew to be Sheriff Passak. Beside him was a woman with hair so tightly coiffed that the pile of it seemed to be more like a helmet than anything as soft as a woman's tresses.

She was observing the group of men pushing, shoving, and yelling at one another. Her face was frozen in disgust. The sheriff and a couple of his men were apparently protecting her. The people on the other side included a well-dressed man and a group of other men dressed in blue police uniforms. The color separated them from the brown-jacketed sheriff's deputies.

Harry couldn't hear what was being said at first. But then the blue-coated men seemed to move in unison, leading the well-dressed civilian up the stairs and onto the stage. He grabbed the microphone that was already set up.

"Men! People! Listen to me!" he screamed into the amplified system. "This is Mayor Dale of Mesa City. This gathering is illegal." The crowd sent up a wave of catcalls.

"Bring on Cecelia!"

"Get the city faggot off the stage!" Whistles and applause broke through the night.

"The sheriff of this county has gone too far. You can't take things into your own hands. There's a question of law."

"This ain't your city. This is county land. Go back to town!" one voice yelled over the others.

As though it was their cue, a dozen brown-uniformed deputies stormed the stage. There were a couple of quick fists thrown. The policemen were ready to take out their guns and confront the deputies, but over the loudspeakers Harry and the rest of the crowd could hear the mayor order, "No! No guns."

The police, their faces showing humiliation and rage, allowed the deputies to lead them off the stage, along with their mayor. To add insult to injury, the deputies handcuffed the officers off to the side, bringing appreciative yells from the crowd.

This was, evidently, a perfect moment for State Senator Range. All of a sudden Harry saw her face break into a smile as rigid as her scowl had been earlier. He was reminded of an aged beauty queen who thought her life was one long running audition for toothpaste commercials.

As soon as she'd gotten onto the stage, the crowd cheered. "Ceel! Ceel! Ceel!" they began to chant. They broke into even louder yells when the woman lifted her arms up high in a victory salute. *"Ceel! Ceel! Ceel!"*

"Let us pray!" the woman said in a loud voice. Harry watched as the face transformed from campaign smile to the mask of a devout woman. She went through some stuff about saving the lives of the dearly beloved and the triumph of good over evil.

The mob was restless while her voice was going on, but they were evidently used to this from their state senator, and they weren't going to interrupt their star.

As soon as she'd said, "Amen," the throng let out a cheer as though she'd just led a pep rally instead of a prayer.

"You know"—the campaign smile was back—"that I have always stood for what is good and right here in this part of our state."

A murmur of agreement went through the crowd.

"You know that I have the utmost respect for the American Constitution."

The noise was louder with accord.

"But you also know that I am a woman of the American West."

The gathering broke into wild applause at that one.

Senator Range leaned into her microphone with a clear physical message that she was going to get serious now. "We have always done what we could to help out our natives. We have always allowed them their reservation, and we have let them have the privilege of Christian education.

"The rest of the country doesn't understand the red men the way we do. They can't see the faults, the inability to coexist with civilized persons. They think that the reservations are a way to protect the red man's way of life. We understand that it is a necessary separation of a people who simply could not live in a civilized environment.

"No, Mayor Dale and his nice eastern-educated lawyer friends think differently. But we know. We *know*!"

Loud applause broke through the ranks.

"This tragedy here at the Piute Mine is proof. This was no accident. We *know*! It proves that the red man can't wait for the wheels of justice to turn. He wants his reward just as a child does, right now. But we *know* that a child must learn discipline. A child must be taught to wait his turn.

"A child must be punished when he does wrong. We *know* that!"

Harry expected another loud agreement. But the mob was content to stand in awed silence. This was getting very dangerous.

"There is no press in Mesa County tonight for a reason. There is no press because they have been excluded. We don't need any eastern liberals coming out here and telling us what to do! We *know* what to do. We *know* a child must be punished for these bombs.

"Mayor Dale can claim all the civil rights he wants . . . tomorrow. Tonight it's time for the men of Mesa County to remember their history, remember the way that justice, real justice—not the liberal mumbo jumbo of courts that would steal men's land from them—should be handed out. A crime has been committed. A terrible crime. Innocent men have been trapped, maybe murdered, in this mine.

"Do you know what else has gone on this night? A group of Coyote Clan have attacked the village of Five Corners. They've left behind five dead white men."

A whisper of shock and anger wove its way through the gathering now.

"They were killed in cold blood as they stood protecting their homes. If it hadn't been for one brave man, they probably would have killed the women and children. One man with a rifle saved a village."

Senator Range let the words sink in. The men were becoming agitated. They didn't know about this killing at Five Corners. But they believed every word that the charismatic politician told them. If the Coyote Clan had really bombed the mine, and if the Coyote Clan had really shot up a village, then were they really the unrestrained villains that Range was saying they were?

Harry watched as a group of men moved through the crowd, stopping every once in a while to encourage, to inflame, to excite. He recognized Ron as one of them. The big Anglo with the blotched skin seemed to be able to pick up on any person who was wavering. He took a calm man or woman, grabbed a shoulder or an arm, and whispered in an ear. By the time he'd left, the face of the individual would be flushed with anger. A quiet voice would become one of the yelling crowd.

"Are the men of this region going to allow only one single man the honor of protecting us from the Coyote Clan? The red men are on their hated warpath. Are you going to sit here and wait for them to attack your homes? Would you like to listen to Mayor Dale some more? Maybe he could tell you the exact manner with which you could read a Coyote Clan man his rights before you defend your wife from rape."

"No, no, no, no!" hundreds of voices screamed in rage.

It was masterful. Harry looked on and saw just what was happening. The tension and the dread of the men waiting for word from the mine was being turned. She was using their anxiety, playing with it, transforming their sense of impotence over their inability to do anything here into a seething hatred.

*"Let's go to the reservation and show the bastards!"*

*"Get to the mesa. That's where the radicals are!"*

The mob was out of control. The men started to race to their cars and trucks. There were too many of them with hunting rifles and shotguns attached to the cabs for Harry to believe. It was nothing less than an armed militia, one without any restraining commander to it. It was an army going out to do battle.

Little Billy Rakin was still clutching his mother's skirt. Harry's own blood was ready to boil. The kid shouldn't be seeing this madness in human beings!

"We going, Harry, are we? It looks like a great fight. Let's go, Harry." Marty was jumping up and down with his usual excitement.

"We're going, Marty. But I think you forgot which side we're on again. We're going to have to have a talk in the car."

Harry saw Ron moving through the crowd with a group of men following him. There were simply too many people for Harry and Marty to track them all. They had to believe and trust that Beeker and Rosie would be doing their part in this operation. You had to trust the rest of a team to carry their weight. The most obvious good they could do was to track the guy they knew was going to be in the midst of trouble.

"Quick, let's get to the car," Harry ordered. They were going to go wherever Ron was headed.

Cowboy landed the Lear Jet with his usual perfection. He taxied the plane to the small terminal at the Mesa City airport. As soon as he'd come to a stop, he moved to the back and helped Adamson open the door, then let down the folding exit stairs.

The executive smiled at him. Cowboy couldn't believe this guy. After all he'd heard over the intercom, he had too good an idea of what Adamson was really like. But the guy was acting as though he was just walking off to a board of directors meeting.

Maria Vasquela left after the boss. She looked at Cowboy with an expression that made it seem as if she were pleased he'd learned his place. She would, obviously, like to have Cowboy doing these domestic chores rather than have to admit he was a pro who held her life in his hands while he was piloting the Lear. "Later, Mr. Hatcher," she said, as though giving the flier an order was too much fun for her to resist.

Cowboy just nodded.

He left the plane after they'd entered the terminal. He followed them inside just in time to see them drive away in an awaiting company limousine. There was a Nevari man in a security uniform nearby. Cowboy walked up to him, smiled. "Takes a lot to get the company president out here in the middle of the night."

"We have a lot going on." The guard smiled. He was enjoying himself. "It's going to be good times for Nevari."

"A mine accident?"

"Hell, that was no accident. Some hot-blooded Indians just signed their own death certificates, is all."

"Yeah," Cowboy said, careful to not stop smiling. He knew two hot-blooded Indians who were not going to die that night, or any other, if he had anything to say about it.

He sauntered over to the airport manager's office. Inside there was only a clerk. "How you doing?" Cowboy said, all friendship.

"Okay. You bring in the Nevari Lear?" The clerk was young, no more than twenty-five. Cowboy figured that he had to be an airport groupie. No one else would take a job that had such terrible hours and little excitement. That kind of person loved being able to throw around brand names.

"Yeah, I'm the big boy on the Nevari fleet. Hey, I can't remember: Do we have other planes here?"

"Oh, sure." The clerk sat up and pulled out a file.

The clerk was overtly pleased with the idea of having a conversation with a real pilot. He quickly went through his papers. "You know, I bet there's one thing here you'd really like. I mean, you got all kinds of little planes for ferrying people to locations and all that, but, well, you must have been in the Air Force, right? I bet you were in 'Nam."

Cowboy looked at the guy and shook his head yes. It was always hard for him to deal with people who wanted to make believe that Vietnam had been some kind of circus, where all the performers got little sticks of candy-covered apples when they were done. The war had been a lot more than that, a lot different. But this wasn't the time to give the kid a history lesson.

"Well, you know, Nevari bought some surplus stuff. There's a Hughes OH-6A here. They bought that Cayuse and revamped it—took out the armament and put in some stuff for geological surveys. I bet that would bring back lots of memories."

Cowboy thought his heart would stop. "You mean there's a 'copter here? Just sitting out there?" He hadn't seen it.

"It's in the Nevari hangar. They don't use it much. Like I say, just for surveys. I bet you'd like to take that baby up."

"Sure as hell would."

"Well, tomorrow you can talk to the manager. He's a vet too. I'm sure he'll let you."

Cowboy looked at the bright-faced clerk. The kid was happy to live something vicariously through Cowboy. He would have to use that. Cowboy leaned over. "I can't take the chance. The president might come back and want to get to LA right away. Hell, I might only have a couple of hours. Come on, kid, I'll just take the keys to the hangar—"

"I can't, mister. Honest, it'd be my job."

"I'll vouch for you. Hell, I'm the one flying the big bird. I'm the hotshot of the fleet. Come on, let's go to the hangar."

The kid hesitated.

"You know, I really want to look at that mesa."

"Oh, that?"

Cowboy noticed that the kid wasn't at all surprised.

"That's what they've been using it for all along. Jeez, I guess if you know all about those surveys, then you must be okay."

Cowboy didn't dare speak or move. Whatever the special open sesame was, he'd just said it.

"But you've never flown there. Here, I'll give you the chart." The kid pulled out a map. "Here it is. There's all kinds of names for it. The Coyote Clan—you know, the local Indians—they think it's holy. But we know what it really is—"

"Sure we do." Cowboy saw the coordinates of the spot the clerk was pointing to. "Come on, kid, I might only have a short while. I used to live in Cayuses. I can't wait."

# 15

Harry had driven up to the reservation village in the dark without his headlights. He hadn't needed them. There was enough moonlight to show the road, and the taillights of the cars in front of him had led the way.

"Get the big boy, Marty," was all the Greek said as he pulled to a stop.

"Hot shit." Appelbaum jumped over the seat and into the back. He quickly prepared his M60 for use. "Ready. Oh, are we ready!"

"Marty, you have to remember whose side you're on. Now, don't forget."

"I'll do just what you told me, Harry. I'll just think about Beak and Tsali all the time. Red man is friend; Anglo is foe. Right? See I'm not dumb."

Harry closed his eyes and, for another countless time, wondered about that. "Let's go. Hold your fire until we know it's necessary."

They took their weapons—Marty had handed Harry the M16 and his ammunition before they got out of the car. The night was cool for this part of the country. There were only a few lights on along the street of the little town. Harry and Marty carefully went around the back of one of the rows of houses.

In the street, through the breaks between the buildings, they could see the crowd of men led by Ron. There were brown-uniformed deputies in the middle of it, but they were a part of the madness; they had no peacekeeping role in this mess.

The crowd seemed to be heading to one of the small wooden shacks. Harry and Marty were standing in the house's shadows when the men came to a standstill. Some of them were holding up flaming torches. It made Harry remember strange and frightening old movies about the South. This was a lynch mob. No doubt about it.

"Pale Fart, get your ass out here!" Ron was leading the way still. He was shouting at someone inside the house.

Harry lifted up his M16. "Get ready, Marty."

The door to the shack opened. A tall man dressed in poor clothes but with the bearing of a leader stepped onto the stairs. "You know my name. It's White Wind."

"Pale Fart's better for a heathen like you. You killed those miners. You and the rest of the tribal council are going to pay for it."

The man was obviously Indian. Harry looked into the crowd and saw that one man had brought a thick length of rope. This *was* a lynch mob. But they weren't going to lynch an Indian while Harry was around. "Cover me," he snapped at Appelbaum.

He walked forward into the light from the doorway. "He isn't going anyplace."

The crowd stopped short at the sight of the big mustached man. The Indian they'd come after was startled as well. But there suddenly seemed to be recognition on his face.

Ron sneered at Harry. "You go after red ass like you do kikes?"

Harry hoped that Marty would keep it together. "Forget it, just forget it," he said. "You guys, just go home. Leave this man alone. He hasn't done anything to you."

The crowd wasn't buying it. Harry swept over them with his eyes and hoped that he'd find some sanity in their midst. Maybe another man to step forward and try to relax them. But it wasn't going to happen.

Harry sighed. This was a situation he found himself in all too often. He kept on wanting to think that people were being duped into things; they were really okay deep inside. Maybe some men were. But he understood, as he had before, that this crowd wanted to be here. They were enjoying it. They wanted to see the Indian hanged. That was too bad. Because it gave him only one recourse.

He made his calculations quickly. White Wind was still staring at him, wondering what the next step would be. Harry was locating the guns. Most of them were Remington .30-.30s, hunting rifles. But they were guns that those men would know intimately. They were rifles they would know how to use.

That meant he had no chance to go easy on the men. He had no way to be nice about all this. *One, two, three!* He counted silently, but when he got to the money number, there was nothing silent at all.

In one quick movement, Harry had pushed White Wind back into the doorway of the house. As he followed the Indian in, Harry was shooting his M16's rounds of ammunition into the night air. But they weren't wild shots. Harry didn't know how to take wild shots.

They were aimed with deadly accuracy. The first two bullets hit Ron and blew away the entire back of his head. Even before the pockmarked man hit the ground, he was dead. So were two of the sheriff's deputies who had stood close to him. Each one had a round of metal in his chest. They'd been thrown back as hard as if they'd been hit by a Miami Dolphins linebacker.

The crowd stood stock-still for a second, then broke, running in every direction. Their minds were suddenly reeling at the sight of three dead men on the dirt road. They had come along to see an Indian swing, maybe to see some others get theirs. They hadn't counted on this deadly resistance.

Inside the house, Harry ran to the front room. He used the butt of his rifle to break open a window. The men on the street weren't just going to go home now, he knew that. They were going to fall back and regroup, regain their madness. Like rabid dogs, they'd been kicked, but the disease was on them. They'd come back—they wouldn't even consider another option.

"You got a gun?" Harry screamed at White Wind.

"Just a .22 for snakes, rabbits," the Indian answered.

Harry had the barrel of his M16 sticking out the window. He looked over his shoulder at the man. He had to close his eyes and open them again. He'd recognized the name, of course. This was Beeker's friend from the Marine Corps. But it was more than a friendship. There was something about White Wind that made him more than the word *friend* could ever describe. There was that combination of Indian and Marine that produced a certain bearing, a certain way of standing stock upright. Underneath those worn clothes and away from the poor surroundings, this was a man who could have stood with Billy Leaps in many places—even today he could be one of the half-breed Cherokee's peers.

"Look, if you're half as good with that .22 as I think you are, you can outshoot all of them. Better get it ready."

The crowd was beginning to reassemble. They were more cautious now. They had some leadership, probably the surviving deputies. They were splitting into four attack groups. They'd assault the house from different directions.

Here it comes, thought Harry. "Hey, take that side window. Pick off the men in the brown uniforms, if you can. They're the brains. They're the ones that are goading them on."

"Got it." White Wind had his small rifle in his hand and went to the opening Harry had pointed to. Harry was going to take the largest of the four cadres, the one that was going to be stupid enough to come at them head-on.

The other two groups of men were off to the right. They would have to be Marty's. He just hoped Appelbaum would remember the lecture on their loyalties that Harry had given him in the car. If he didn't . . . *You had to trust the team.*

A man like Harry really does try to find the best in people. The two dozen men in the group he'd taken for himself began their rush, and Harry gave them every chance. He took out two more deputies first. Didn't they want to go home now? No, they kept on coming. That left him no more options. His M16 sang out, and the rounds went through the semiautomatic rifle with horrible precision. The men went down until the survivors realized just how naked and vulnerable they were. They stopped. Harry wished them backward. They wouldn't go. There was one of them standing in the middle. He was giving out some kind of rebel yell to get the men to continue. Harry took aim and sent a bullet into his forehead.

That, at least, convinced some of the others to run for shelter. It also gave Harry time to reload for their return if they insisted on suicide.

He could tell what else was going on by the sounds. Off to the one side there were the *pings* of the .22. Harry, with his M16 ready, moved over to see what White Wind was doing. He had only a half dozen men coming at his window. Two of them were on the ground. The others, with better cover from the neighboring house, were taking shots at White Wind. The bullets were breaking the glass panes of the window, sending showers of glass slivers into the room. There was blood on White Wind's head; Harry assumed, *hoped*, the blood was just from the flying glass.

Harry stuck his rifle out the window. He pulled off about ten rounds and saw four bodies sprawl on the ground.

He was calm. Not because of his own ability but because of the other sounds reverberating through the building. It was the mortal choir of Appelbaum's M60. The huge and horrible weapon was working overtime.

Harry could follow it as it moved up the alleyway. Marty and his one true love were coming out the front. The men in front of Rosie and White Wind heard it too. They knew it meant even more danger than they'd already faced. They just didn't know how much more danger.

Harry pulled White Wind away from the window. "It'll be all over soon."

The chorus of metal sang; the air rent with the passage of molten steel as it moved through the night. The sounds continued in a pattern. They were in the front of the house now. They were right in front of Harry's window.

The Greek crawled over to that place and looked out. Appelbaum was in front of him. The impossibly large machine gun was roaring. Men were desperately trying to escape its certain deliverance of execution. They were all caught as they ran down the rutted dirt road. One by one they jumped up, most often to have their dead or dying bodies dance to the tune of Marty and his gun as the rounds continued to slam into them.

Screams of death, prayers of forgiveness, promises of revenge all shot through the night. But the bullets kept on coming, and they didn't know what it was to forgive or to forget; they could only take their vengeance.

Marty took a full turn and faced those men who had been seeking shelter from Harry and White Wind. From his new position, they were open, wide open, to receive the last deadly blast of the M60.

Then it was over. Marty let the M60's barrel slump till it pointed to the ground. He looked over to Harry and gave the all clear sign. Then he smiled. Mission accomplished.

All that was left were the dead bodies of the fools who had lost their senses and tried to take out a friend of the Black Berets.

Over on the horizon, Harry could see the first signs of dawn. The new day was starting. He sat back on the floor and wondered what would happen next.

# 16

The same sunrise was shining on Beeker. His higher elevation gave him a slightly earlier preview of the day. But his wasn't a brighter outlook. He was sitting cross-legged on the edge of the mesa, near the spot where the one good road wound its way to the tabletop.

He felt a hand on his shoulder. Tsali. He turned and looked at his son. Like himself, Tsali was dressed for the battle. They had on the camouflage pants and shirts of the Black Berets. Their web belts, their boots, all of it was in top shape. The way it always was with the team.

The ritual of preparing for the coming battle had been shared by father and son. There was only one more element to handle. Tsali had it in his hands. It was cammy grease. Billy Leaps smiled. "We'll do it as though we were the old people," he said.

He took the can from Tsali's hand and opened it. He reached in and covered the tips of his fingers with the stuff. Then he smeared one long horizontal line of coloring over the top of Tsali's cheekbones, leaving a single trail from one ear to the other, crossing over the top of the boy's nose. Beeker repeated the motion.

For a moment, he thought he *was* one of the old people. He thought this must be what it was like to put on the war paint for your son when he was going to his first battle. But he remembered that it wasn't so. This wasn't the first time that Tsali would be fighting with the men. There had been other times, so many other times for a youngster of seventeen.

"We'll only do that. The camouflage isn't going to do any good in this country. But the grease will cut the glare from the sun that reflects off your skin. It will make it easier to see."

Tsali looked at Beeker for a moment—there was only seriousness in him. His hands moved. Beeker answered, "Yes, like the football players."

Tsali was young enough to think of sportsmen even at a time like this one. But he wasn't so distracted that he forgot the importance of what they were doing. He took the can from his father's hands and reached in with his own fingers. Just as Beeker had done to him, Tsali left one long line of grease on his father's face.

The two of them almost never touched, and certainly not with this kind of intimacy. As Beeker felt the fingers move on his flesh, as he realized that it was his own son preparing him for this fight, he felt an urge to shed tears. It was an uncommon one, but it was one that had come more often with Tsali than with anyone else on earth.

Beeker swallowed hard and then stood. Tsali, not admitting that anything special had happened, busied himself with recapping the grease can.

"Let's go to the others."

They walked to the middle of the camp. The same old women were cooking the same breakfast, but they were doing it with a seriousness the two Cherokee hadn't seen on the mesa until now.

Like their ancestors, these women were doing their part to

prepare their men for war. One of them looked up and, with a start, covered her mouth to squelch a scream as she looked at the two of them. It was the paint—the cammy grease was too much like the war paint of the old people. It was like looking at the dead come to protect their children.

"A truck's coming!" a voice called out from the side of the mesa.

The fifteen Coyote Clan men stood up. Each one had some kind of weapon in his hands. Most of them were only hunting rifles. Small Eagle only had a compound bow. It was going to be bad if these were the only tools the Coyote Clan had to fight off the growing numbers of vigilantes ready to storm the mesa.

Beeker and the others went back to the spot he'd just vacated, where they could see the road. "Just one truck, probably another of your people," Billy Leaps said to Small Eagle.

They watched the progress of the pickup as it made its way up the steep incline. Beeker had his rifle ready, a .30-.30 hunting rifle from one of the stores. Just in case, he told himself. One lone truck could look so helpless but could be so deadly.

The truck made its way to the top. As soon as it did, Tsali broke into a run. He was the first to see the driver. He pulled open the door to the cab. "Hey, boy, how you doing?" Rosie said. He stepped out and let Tsali grab hold of his bare chest. "Easy," he said through clenched teeth. "Real easy, kid. I'm hurt."

Tsali sprang backward. He was horrified at the idea he could have harmed one of the men.

Silver Cloud forced her way through the cluster of men and went over to Rosie. "Let me see. What's wrong?"

She'd designated herself as the nurse for the crew. Rosie looked at her and got his smile back.

"Honey, there's lots wrong, but little you couldn't take care of."

"What is it?" Beeker was standing next to him now, and he

wasn't interested in any of Rosie's banter. While Silver Cloud was delicately removing the makeshift bandage Rosie had used to stanch the loss of blood from the flesh wound he'd taken, the black man, his face occasionally contorting in pain when Silver Cloud's movements were too much for him, gave a report.

"We heard all about most of it. I couldn't figure it all out, but they made it sound like your buddies back there were Five Corner residents."

"Hell no. But there is some good come of it all. I got a few of their rifles—Mini-14s—brought them with me."

"We can use them. Come on," he said to Small Eagle. "Let's get this truck in position. With my car and a couple of other vehicles, we can create a blockade." They all hurried to line the road with the cars and the truck.

Then it was time to wait. Always wait—the warrior's worst enemy was the horrible and slow passage of time. The sun had risen fully, and the heat was intolerable. Sweat stuck their clothing to their bodies. Beeker wanted to pull off his shirt at one point, to get rid of the clammy sensation. But he knew that sun like this would be too dangerous, even with his Indian coloring.

Then they could see the line of vehicles coming up the roadway. Beeker watched it, now hating the slow motion the cars seemed to be in. They looked like toys at first, getting more life-sized as they approached.

They halted and someone got out of the lead car. He waited, standing there and staring up at the mesa. Beeker couldn't figure out what was going on. Then he saw that someone was bringing on a handheld loudspeaker. It was given to the man. He seemed to be wearing a brown uniform.

"You! Up there!" The man spoke slowly so the echoes of his amplified voice wouldn't lose his words. "Surrender! This is Sheriff Mike Passak!"

Beeker looked at Small Eagle. The Native American Crusade leader spoke: "This is inside the boundaries of even the old reservation. He doesn't have any authority here. We have the right to resist him."

Beeker looked back down at the man. He'd hate to take on a civilian. But this guy must be one of the ones those youngsters Sam and Jack had talked about. The rabble in the area had gathered around the leaders who wanted Indian blood. They were the type of men who weren't following authority—they weren't good citizens being duped by false leaders. They were reaching out for a chance to take on the Indians, get rid of the court claims, all of it just for a day's sporting event.

He took a pair of binoculars he had and swept the line of cars. Every so often he'd find another of the brown uniforms like Passak's. But the men surrounding them weren't the innocents; they were blood hungry—Beeker could see it even from this distance.

"We fight," he said.

"Man, these are even worse odds than I'm used to," Rosie announced. But the black man wasn't complaining, just calmly stating a fact.

Beeker had taken one of the spare Mini-14s. Tsali had grabbed another of the compound bows. *My son, armed with bow and arrow.* Beeker looked down at the line of armed men. There were at least two hundred. He wondered what the odds had been when the Coyote Clan had first defended this mesa.

Then there was a sound. *Whomp, whomp, whomp . . .* It grew quickly louder. Beeker and Rosie looked up in the air. They couldn't believe it. But it was! A 'copter. If the goons down below had airpower as well, they were going to have an even harder time.

Beeker was ready to shoot at the bird. He rolled over on his back and took aim. He saw the Nevari Minerals logo and became more certain it was the enemy. He sighted his Mini-14, trying to gauge the distance. He looked through the sight and studied the plane. There was a hand, waving out the cockpit. Beeker wondered what the hell it was doing. There was something in the hand. A bomb? That small? He squinted, then reached for the binoculars again. He looked up and then broke into wild laughter.

"What the fuck is wrong with you? Are you losing it?" Rosie declared.

"No, no. It's Cowboy."

Beeker had seen what was in the hand. It was the one perfect identifying article: a pair of sunglasses.

The 'copter landed on the mesa, the rotary blades sending clouds of dust over the group. As soon as the motor was turned off, Cowboy jumped out of the craft and ran over to the other Berets. Loud greetings went through the group. There wasn't time to explain to Small Eagle and the rest of them. Beeker and Rosie had to get all the information they could out of the flier.

"One group headed for the reservation village," Beeker said. "We know that. I don't know what happened to them. But this is the main force."

"Well, we gotta take them out," Cowboy responded. "Doesn't seem like much of a problem. Now, if they were going to be fools and lay siege to the mesa, that would be one thing. Your asses would be theirs . . . eventually. But they don't have that kind of time, I bet. Not from what I heard. Even if they did, we got the air now. I think we should just use it and get this place cleared out."

Beeker agreed. "Cowboy, you take up Rosie and me with these Minis. We'll take enough potshots to get rid of them. Rosie, go after the brown uniforms. They're the ones causing all the trouble."

"This little Cayuse isn't exactly like a limousine, you know."

"We'll improvise."

The three men climbed on board. "Rosie, you shoot that thing off too close to my ear and I'll be as deaf as Tsali is mute," Cowboy said.

"Then cover your delicate horns, asshole. I got a lot of singing to do with this baby. The magazines can only hold forty rounds as it is, so you don't have much to worry about. You'll get some rest. Just think how bad it'd be if this was Marty and his M60 girlfriend."

Rosie smiled and slammed a magazine into the rifle. The 'copter rotors roared and quickly lifted the machine up off the ground.

The Cayuse lifted up and then tilted, racing toward the edge of the mesa and the enemy below. The men on the basin floor hadn't known what to make of the 'copter. Even as it came toward them now, they weren't sure. But the first swing the bird made told them more than they had to know. The semiautomatic Mini-14s blasted out their quick rounds. The first target, they'd agreed, was the sheriff. Passak had caused them too much grief. He was staring at the helicopter, wondering what the hell it was all about. He was still straining his neck when the first bullets tore through his chest. With both Rosie and Beeker taking their marksmen aim, the sheriff had been hit with a dozen bullets, at least. They didn't just cut him up, and they didn't just wound him—they exploded his chest.

The other men, now that they saw the intent of the 'copter, ran for cover. Cowboy made another pass. Beeker and Rosie aimed again, shooting for the brown uniforms that were still visible. One after another heavy rounds of the NATO 5.56 mm rounds tore the brown uniforms open and apart.

Rosie began to yell with joy. The sheer exhilaration of the battle was sending his body's chemicals through his system. *"More, baby, more!"* But they'd ended their fourth sweep, and the men on the ground were running now, trying to get their cars started and moving in the other direction, away from the mesa.

"Let 'em go," Beeker said, yelling to be heard over the motor's roar. "Let's get to the village. We have to see what happened to White Wind."

Rosie might have been displeased with the action, but as always, he didn't argue. They were in a fight, and Beeker was in charge. If the man said they had to go on to another firefight, he'd get his jollies there. He watched as Beeker pointed the direction to Cowboy. He'd wait. There'd be more soon.

"I should have known. Damn it, I should have known." Rosie was staring at the streets of the reservation village. They were empty. The last of the ambulances was taking away the wounded and the dead.

Marty was smirking. "We didn't need you flying in and waking up the babies. They were all napping."

"Don't talk about babies!" Harry said.

They stared at him. Harry always looked so sad; they were used to it, but there was something even worse about him right now. Whatever was causing it, they knew they weren't going to argue with his command.

Beeker was off to the side, talking to White Wind. When they'd finished, he came back to the waiting Berets. "The state police are in place. They're taking care of everything from now on. White Wind says they'll do it. Come on, let's get out of here. I want to go back to the motel. Cowboy, you take the 'copter and pick up Tsali. We'll take White Wind's car and meet you back there." Beeker gave the flier directions.

"Your daddy's all calm and relaxed, kid. Everything's going to be okay. You just wait and see. It's all new again." Tsali was staring out the window of the 'copter as it approached the Mesa City airport. "In a little while, we'll be back at the motel, and I'll slip some rum into your Coke. We'll find a lady, two of them, one for me, one for you . . ."

Cowboy babbled on, but the boy kept on looking out the window. The flier finally laid off. There were times when Tsali needed to shut it all out. Cowboy knew that. He knew it perfectly well.

The helicopter landed on the dime. He switched off the rotor. Tsali grabbed his bow and his quiver and the knapsack that held his few things and got out his side.

Cowboy was out the door on the terminal side of the bird. He was walking toward the building when he stopped short. Adamson! With Vasquela. "Just in time," Adamson pulled a .38 from his jacket. "We were wondering where you were, you bastard. On the other side the whole time, weren't you?"

"How could he have faked it all?" Maria asked. She had her own nice little ladylike derringer in her hand. "You get a nice assignment, in any event, Mr. Hatcher. That Lear Jet—it turns out you're the only one who can fly it here. We have a plan for you. One that takes you all the way to Brazil."

Adamson motioned Cowboy over in the direction of the plane. He was still staring at the flier when there was a sudden *twang*. The gasp of air that Maria Vasquela released was the only sound.

Adamson couldn't make a sound, because the full length of an aluminum arrow shaft had pierced his heart.

Maria was stunned at first. She'd dropped her gun a bit, letting it point at the ground. But she recovered before Cowboy could race the distance to grab her. "You bastard," she hissed. She lifted the weapon again, not thinking to worry about the source of the arrow. There was only one thing on her mind—the blond pilot who'd ruined everything.

Cowboy was sure he was going to meet his maker this time. The little gun was so devious, so tiny looking. He prayed she'd be a bad shot; he hoped it'd just lodge a bullet in his shoulder, then he could—

*Twang.*

Now Maria screamed out loud. She had a reason to. Another of those aluminum arrows had found its mark. This one was lodged directly in the center of her wrist.

They didn't notice the decorations of the motel bar. They didn't care about them. Rosie cared about the bourbon he was drinking. If Beeker came in and noticed how much alcohol they were all consuming, he wasn't about to argue right now. Cowboy was over in a corner talking very distinctly and seriously with Tsali. He thought it was just great that the kid was such a fine gentleman, but he sincerely hoped that the next time the boy found *anyone* pointing a lethal weapon at Cowboy's body that he wouldn't take the chance, wonderful shot that he was, at missing such a small target as a lady's wrist.

Rosie ordered another bourbon and realized he had had so much that he didn't give a shit if Marty was repeating the same story for the third time. He could barely follow it, in any event.

Beeker came in and sat down at the table with Rosie and Marty. Tsali and Cowboy joined them, Cowboy continuing to assure the younger man that chivalry was not dead, but had its limits when a lady was holding a gun on someone's best friend.

"It's set. We can go home now," Beeker announced.

"What's set? What's okay? What—" Cowboy and the rest of them wanted answers, not just quick assurances.

"The Coyote Clan claim. It's fine. This was one of the ugliest things I've been through, but the Coyote Clan will be okay.

"Turns out that that woman senator, Range? She was one of the major stockholders of Nevari. She was the brains behind the whole thing. She's going to get the book thrown at her.

"The idea was to isolate the county, get the kind of men

together who would like to go and shoot up some Coyote Clan ass, enough of it that there wouldn't be anyone with guts enough—or brains enough—to follow up on the court case.

"The claim is even more important than we thought. There were more minerals, worth even more than we knew. And it was the water—the water is worth a fortune."

"Is that what Adamson and Vasquela were talking about?"

"No," Beeker said. "That was something else." He smiled over that. "Those were a pair though. Vasquela sang the whole song to the state police. Seems like Nevari was a criminal company. Every one of the major executives had been caught pulling some kind of white-collar crime. Vasquela had a habit of adding extra people to the payroll in her last job. All of them seemed to be her relatives, and they didn't particularly like to come to work. Adamson had broken every rule in the book about toxic dumping where he used to work."

"Why weren't they jailed?" Rosie wanted to know.

"'Cause all those types take care of themselves. If the companies had blown the whistle on their employees, then the companies would have paid the fines as well. They just like to whisk everything under the rug. That's all. Just get rid of it.

"Range knew all that. She's as rich as she was devious. She went out to hire the worst offenders. Just like she made sure that Passak got elected sheriff and that he hired some of the most crooked deputies he could find. She'd spent years setting this up. All to make sure that Nevari wouldn't have to worry about little inconveniences like the law.

"This was a fiefdom. The city officials knew it, but they didn't have any way to stop it. It was beyond their ability. Even when Passak started to do stuff like scare off some local camera crews, the mayor didn't have a way to handle it. Actually, he and his police officers were pretty brave to show up at that rally.

"Range and Passak and Adamson were all set. They were going to let a few of the men go after the Coyote Clan. That'd end that chapter in the book. There aren't that many of the tribe left, remember. Even White Wind knew that. It's why he was so willing to compromise on so many things.

"They figured if they could get a free hand for a couple of days, blow up the mine with some men in it to rile up the crowd, make them nervous, no coverage from the press, that was perfect. Range had most of them tied up with a false lead on a big story. There aren't that many camera crews in a place like this. The rest? 'Detained for their own safety' by the sheriff.

"No witnesses but the offenders. No filmed record. A massacre of the Indians, and who'd really care later on if a few red men didn't win a strange court case after all?"

"But what was this geological thing?" Cowboy said. "Come on, Beeker, there must have been something more. Even a bad company like Nevari could have seen that they could negotiate their way to some agreement with the Coyote Clan. Why did they have to go so far?" Cowboy was onto something—he was sure of it. There was more here.

"It's our secret." Beeker smiled. "It's our nest egg."

"Come on, Billy Leaps, out with it!" the flier demanded. "You know damn well that we have the biggest nest egg we ever dreamed about already."

"Well, if you guys ever find that we just don't have the resources to do something for one reason or another, I got some presents for each and every one of you, and one for Tsali too."

He pulled out official-looking documents and passed one to each of the men.

"Shares in the Coyote Clan Mining Company?" Cowboy looked up. "I don't get it."

"The mesa," Beeker said. "It's nearly solid gold, the richest ore in North America. It was the mountain the conquistadores were looking for.

"It's sacred ground though. White Wind isn't letting on to anyone but a couple of the people from the Native American Crusade, ones who are overly protective of the old ways. Why else do they have so much money if they can't protect that religious ground? They've nearly starved to death for centuries while they were sitting on the wealth. They just didn't know it. Probably if their ancestors had, they wouldn't have touched it anyhow."

They were all stunned. Cowboy looked at the piece of paper with his own name carefully printed on it. "Can we ever do anything that doesn't make us rich?"

No one answered. Beeker spoke: "Guess we take commercial flights back. We can get a commuter flight out of Mesa City, then fly to Shreveport from Las Vegas. Where's Harry? We might as well get going."

Cowboy looked up, as though Harry's name was the only thing that could keep him from memorizing every single letter on the certificate he was holding.

"He's out spending money some place. A hell of a lot of it."

They all looked puzzled. "Don't ask me. I'm just your accountant. It's your dough. Harry wanted some; I went to the local bank with him and got all the numbers and the funds transferred. He can do anything he wants with it. It just seemed like a hell of a lot of money to be using on tourist shit."

# 17

Lydia Rakin opened the door to her ranch house. There was a large man standing there. He looked awfully uncomfortable.

"You couldn't even let his body get cold before you served the papers on the house, could you?" She spat out the words. "For God's sake, I have two kids. I can't make these payments on the mortgage. I know I have to give up the place, but couldn't you—"

"Hey, it's the man from the mine." Billy Rakin broke through his mother's guard at the door and stared up at Harry.

"Hi," the Greek said. Then he looked down at the thick envelope in his hands. He swallowed hard and finally looked at Lydia. "The . . . accident, you know it wasn't one. I'm sure there are ways a good lawyer can get you some money from whatever's left over from Nevari."

He handed Lydia the paper. "That's until then, I mean . . . no, that's for you now. You don't have to worry about paying it back. You can't, since I won't tell you how. I won't tell you where to."

Lydia took the package from Harry. The man was sweating heavily. He looked much worse now than he did at the disaster site. Once Billy had pointed it out, she saw that it was the man they'd talked to.

She ripped open the seal. Inside was her house mortgage.

"You paid it off?" She couldn't believe it.

"Yeah. All of it. You don't have to leave: No one's going to evict you. There's some cash too. To tide you over. Until the court settlement. You know, that can take time."

As though he had to do something physical, Harry reached over suddenly and scooped Billy up into his arms. The little blond boy reached and played with the Greek's thick mustache.

"Will I have one like that?" the boy asked.

"He doesn't really understand . . . yet." Lydia was trying to explain Billy's playfulness. "I don't understand *this*!" She was fanning a wad of thousand-dollar bills. They were mint fresh, and it was just sinking in that there were even more than she had thought possible.

"Don't . . . I mean, don't worry about it."

"You weren't on their side. This isn't blood money. Why are you doing this?"

"Lady, look, I . . . I just want the boy to be okay. I don't want him to . . ." Harry never was good with words.

Harry set Billy down. "Mister, will I look like you when I grow up? With a mustache like that?"

Harry looked down. "No, no, you're going to look like your daddy. You remember, he was a good man. You told me once you wanted to grow up to be just like him. You do that, you hear me?"

The Greek turned then and walked to his rental car. He had to wait a minute before he turned the key. He thought he might cry.

But he didn't. He just felt a little bit more weight on his heart. There was already a lot. He hadn't forgotten much in this life. He just kept on thinking one thing.

*Kids shouldn't have to know about this . . .*